HOME FOR CHRISTMAS...

Suddenly I was thinking about my dad and how I hadn't spent many Christmases with him. We've never really connected, but as far as family goes, he's all I have left. That's when I burst into tears—a forty-two-year-old successful Realtor, crying her eyes out on her Pottery Barn couch. I sat there, thinking about how this year, if I didn't go home, I'd be alone. I don't have a boyfriend. Truth be known, I haven't had a date in a year because I work too much and I'm picky as hell about the men I date.

Long story short—I bought an airline ticket online. Deep down, I was hoping I might get closer to my father over Christmas.

Then I called him.

Mary Schramski

began writing when she was about ten. The first story she wrote took place at a junior high school. Her mother told her it was good, so she immediately threw it away. She read F. Scott Fitzgerald at eleven, fell in love with storytelling and decided to teach English. She holds a Ph.D. in creative writing and enjoys teaching and encouraging other writers. She lives in Nevada with her husband, and her daughter who lives close by.

Visit Mary's Web site at www.maryschramski.com.

the LIGHTHOUSE

MARY SCHRAMSKI

THE LIGHTHOUSE

copyright © 2005 Mary L. Schramski

i s b n 0 3 7 3 8 8 0 6 9 3

This edition published by arrangement with Harlequin Books S.A.

® and TM are trademarks of the publisher. Trademarks indicated with
® are registered in the United States Patent and Trademark Office, the
Canadian Trade Marks Office and in other countries.

TheNextNovel.com

 HARLEQUIN®

PRINTED IN U.S.A.

From the Author

Dear Reader,

I was inspired to write *The Lighthouse* because I believe:

- There are people in our lives who guide us through the rough times,

- Lighthouses are special,

- And no matter what problems we face, there is always hope.

I also love the sound of the ocean in the morning, the veil of fog as the sun breaks through the clouds at sunrise and the happiness I feel when I connect with my family. *The Lighthouse* is the story of how a family deals with love, grief, past hurts—and how the light of forgiveness can bring us home, as a lighthouse does.

Come with me. We'll stroll the beach, watch the sun set, laugh, cry and believe!

Mary

For my daughter
Jess—my light.

CHAPTER 1

The stars and the rivers
And waves call you back.

—Pindar

I feel invisible right now.

I'm sitting on an airplane next to an older man who reminds me a little of my father. And we are waiting to deplane into the Los Angeles airport. We never spoke a word to each other. At thirty thousand feet, when it got really bumpy, I wanted to say to him, Wow this is scary, but he was reading and I didn't want to bother him.

Not saying what I feel isn't unusual for me. Even when I have my feet on the ground, I don't tell people what I think.

Like three weeks ago when I was watching TV. A Christmas commercial about cameras came on.

In the middle, where the smiling, tearful mother says goodbye to her daughter, I started thinking about my mom, how I miss her, and how I wish I'd told her I loved her the last time we spoke.

Suddenly, I was thinking about my dad and how I hadn't spent many Christmases with him. We've never really connected, but as far as family goes, he's all I have left. That's when I burst into tears—a forty-two-year-old, successful Realtor, crying her eyes out on her Pottery Barn couch. Twice I stopped, then I'd think about my mother, alone, in her smashed-up silver Camry. I'd start crying again. She called me the night before her accident. I didn't call her back because I was angry about a million-dollar house I'd missed signing.

That night, after the commercial and tears, I sat on the couch thinking about how this year, if I didn't go home, I'd be alone. I don't have a boyfriend. Truth be known, I haven't had a date in a year because I work too much and I'm picky as hell about the men I date.

Long story short, I bought an airline ticket online. Deep down, I was hoping I might get closer to my father over Christmas.

Then I called him.

He sounded surprised to hear from me, and when I told him I was coming home for Christmas, there was this long pause. He said, *That's not such a good idea. I have to go.*

Click.

I stared at the phone, felt confused, then I got mad. My own father telling me not to come home for Christmas! I stomped around the house, threw a pillow across the room. Then when I thought about how my mother always let out a whoop when I told her I could make it home for the holidays, I started crying again.

I finally got control, but it took a while. I was holding my breath, trying to get rid of a mean case of hiccups and telling myself as soon as they went away I was going to call my father back and ask him what in the hell was wrong. That's when the phone rang.

I said hello, and Dad launched into this explanation about how I woke him up. I looked at my watch, didn't believe him, yet didn't say anything. He asked what time he should pick me up at the airport. I got more confused, but I still didn't say anything. None of this was like him. Instead of asking him what was really wrong, I gave him my itinerary and here I am, waiting to walk into the LAX terminal.

The airplane door must have opened because people are grabbing bags and inching down the aisle.

The man next to me smiles, leans a little closer. "Have a nice holiday," he says.

I smile back. "You, too."

He gets up, walks down the aisle in front of me.

When I reach the terminal, I take a deep breath. It's late and the terminal is almost empty. I go down to the baggage-claim area. I see my father right away. He's standing by the far wall, arms crossed with that familiar, serious look on his face. His hair's a little grayer than I remember, and his blue shirt doesn't match his brown pants, which surprises me because he's always been a neat dresser.

As I walk over, he sees me, smiles, steps forward.

"Christine," he says in the same deep, calm voice I've heard all my life.

"Hi, Dad." I hesitate, want to hug him, but I'm still a little miffed about the phone call. I give him a quick hug, then pull back. "It's good to see you."

"Same here. Are you ready?" he asks, then looks at my roller bag. "This all you have?"

I nod, take the handle of the suitcase, and we begin walking.

"Flight okay?"

"The landing almost knocked out one of my fillings."

Dad smiles. We've talked this airplane talk for a long time. That's one of the first memories I have of my father. Him standing over my bed in his smooth, dark blue pilot uniform, and Mom saying, *Good night, have a good flight.* I probably giggled because of the rhyme.

"How's work?" he asks as we make our way toward the exit door.

"Busy. Really busy. I've got a lot of house sales coming up. One big one." I've always tried to impress him. People have called me a workaholic, and it was a big stretch for me to leave all my listings right now, but after I bought the ticket and called Dad, I didn't have a choice.

He stops right before we walk out the door. "Can you afford to be away from work from now till New Year's Day?"

The man behind us trips a little over my suitcase. My father puts his hand on my back, moves me to the side, out of the way.

"Sure. Christmas week is really slow, nothing will happen. I've worked hard all year. I deserve a little break. I'm the office's top seller."

"As long as you're not losing money. We'll play it by ear. If you have to go back early, I'll understand."

"Nobody buys a house around Christmas." This isn't exactly true—a listing can sell anytime. I lean closer, give him a quick hug. "I'll handle everything when I get home. I'm a master at real estate sales." I doubt if my father cares about this fact. He wanted me to go to college and become a doctor or lawyer, but I didn't want to. We had a lot of fights over this. And it didn't make it any better that I wasn't settled until six years ago, when I finally found something I'm good at.

We walk outside.

"I had to park far away."

"Parking at the Tucson airport is terrible, too." I fill my lungs with moist air. The scent of the ocean brings a memory of my mother sitting on the back porch step, her head held back, lips parted. She takes a deep breath and smiles at me.

My heart begins to ache.

"Those bastards. President has to do more."

"What?" I look at him. We're walking past the corded-off, empty parking spaces.

"President needs to do more about security," Dad says, gesturing toward the spaces. The irritation I hear in his voice surprises me and I feel achy and tired.

Dad settles my carry-on in the trunk of his Volvo and opens the passenger door. His car is immaculate, as usual. I glance down. A list stands at attention in the cup holder: *bread, milk, gas, 8:15 Christine*. I laugh.

"Something funny?" Dad asks as he climbs in.

"Your list."

"Yeah?"

"You put me on the list. Would you have forgotten me if you hadn't?" I'm kidding, but then remember the other night when he told me he didn't want me to come home. Yet he's always been a list-maker, a dependable man.

"Of course not. Just a habit."

He starts the car, maneuvers out of the parking lot, and soon we're on the 405. Air rushes in through his open window. I open mine, breathe in, feel as if I'm washing the last bit of arid desert out of my lungs.

Dad sighs.

A memory of my mother sneaks in. I close my eyes, relax. Warm afternoon sunlight streaming onto the back porch, my mother acting silly, telling me I can drink air. Me, a giggly girl. I hold my head back, sip the cool breeze. Dad asks what we're doing, and in my little-girl voice I tell him *drinkin' air*. He sighs, shakes his head and explains to my mother she shouldn't fill my head with nonsense.

I look over at him. He's driving like he always has, right hand on the steering wheel, the other resting on his left thigh. Some things about him I know well.

"So everything's okay? You don't mind having company this week?"

He glances over, then back to the road. "Of course not. Why should I mind? Everything okay with you?"

"I was just wondering. You know, well, you hung

up on me." I feel the anger I felt in my living room, but I push it back so I don't have to feel it right now.

"I was tired." He stares straight ahead.

For some reason, I don't believe him and I want him to explain more, say something else, yet I know he won't. "But you're okay?"

"Fine. How's work?" he asks again.

"Great. I'll probably win top sales for the office this year. I'm the top seller." I repeat what I just told him. I work fourteen-hour days, but to produce the way I do, I have to. Most of the time, I'm exhausted. "What have you been up to?"

"Managing to keep busy."

"Doing what?"

He flips on his turn signal and eases into the right lane to pick up the 110. "I've got lots of things to do, taking care of the house, for one thing. It's getting older by the day. So your flight was okay?"

"Fine. A little crowded, but since it's two days before Christmas I expected that." I drink in more air, wishing I felt as if I could open up, tell him he pissed me off when I called to tell him about my trip, but I can't.

"Yeah, it's crazy flying at this time," Dad says.

"People want to be home for the holidays."

Dad looks at me, then back to the road. "I'm glad you're home. That you could take the time off from work."

"Thanks. I didn't want you to be alone." My shoulders relax a little and I lean back. Before I became a Realtor, I used to jump from job to job—waitress, secretary, Pottery Barn sales clerk. With those jobs, I could come home every year if Mom sent me airfare. My father used to just shake his head when I'd tell him I'd changed jobs again. Then one day, a friend said I should try selling houses because I had a knack for making people happy. I didn't know what the heck she meant by that since my life was pretty much a train wreck. I was in debt, not happy with any job and never found a relationship that worked.

When I asked her what she meant, she said I was *nice*. I laughed, told her I wished I wasn't so nice. That was seven years ago, and three top sales awards later.

"Still like your job?" Dad asks.

"The job's great. The other day, a client told me

I helped her find her dream home. That really reminded me of Mom."

An eye blink later, he turns the steering wheel sharply to change lanes and brakes squeal. I'm thrown forward toward the dashboard.

"Good God!"

A horn screeches and I glance back, thinking he's caused a ten-car pile up on the 110, but everything's okay.

"Dad, you cut that guy off."

"He had plenty of room. People should learn how to drive!"

A weird feeling spirals through me. This isn't like him at all, but neither is him hanging up on me. I look over at him. Basically, he's the same, maybe a little thinner, grayer. I turn my attention to the window, watch as we drive through the oil fields, come all the way up Pacific Avenue and turn right on Thirty-eighth Street.

When Dad turns into the driveway of our house, my heart jumps a little. It's the one I grew up in, the one my mother loved, decorated, the one she didn't come back to eight months ago.

* * *

We walk on the sidewalk that cuts from the garage to our house through the night-wet grass. I'm in front pulling my suitcase, and Dad is right behind me. The night is so quiet I can hear his shoes tapping against the concrete.

I scuff my feet against the familiar flowery welcome mat on the back porch. Dad unlocks the door, flips on the light, motions me to go in, and I step into my mother's kitchen.

"I'll put your suitcase in your room." Dad disappears through the swinging door that leads from the kitchen to the rest of the house.

My head is aching, I guess from the flight, the drive home, anticipation. I glance around. The same familiar yellow walls—*like sunshine*—was how my mother described the color years ago. My dad told her that was silly.

I was so looking forward to seeing familiar things, but now I'm not so sure. When I'm in Tucson, I can keep my grief tucked away. Nothing there reminds me of home, and I'm so busy most of the time, I don't have time to think about anything but work.

Yet, right now, it feels like just yesterday that I

sat at the oak table in the kitchen in shocked disbelief that my mother was gone. Dad has changed nothing. The white-and-yellow tile and the turquoise art deco canisters sitting by the stove are still the same. And the white curtains edge the window over the sink. Except now the room is a mess with unwashed dishes, a greasy frying pan on the stove.

The old refrigerator, squat as an old woman, hums. I place my purse on the table in the middle of the room, dig around, find the little foil packet of Aleves in my makeup bag. The door to the dining room swings wide, Dad walks in, and the refrigerator sighs.

"Need anything?" he asks.

"No." A half lie. I'm not sure what I need. I feel numb—a little disoriented, but I don't know how to tell him this. And he probably wouldn't understand, anyway. I glance toward the dining room and, for a split second, I expect my mom to push through the swinging door, hug me, then sit at the table and pat the space beside her.

My headache deepens.

"I saw Sandra this morning. She's looking forward to seeing you," Dad says.

Sandra is three years older than I am, and she grew up in the house next door. We played together when we were young and, when she went to high school, I followed her like a puppy, entranced by the boys, makeup and dates that swirled around her. Three years ago, she moved back into her childhood home to take care of her mother. We've kept in touch, but over the last few years I've been so busy, we haven't talked much.

"I'll go over tomorrow. It's too late now."

Dad looks at the clock. "Better turn on the news."

"Still on at nine?"

We both look toward the yellow sunflower clock over the fridge, and I laugh despite what I'm feeling. Eight-fifty-five.

"Yep, still on at nine. Are you coming?" he throws over his shoulder as he walks out of the kitchen.

"I'll be there in a minute."

A moment later the TV blares. I walk to the refrigerator, open the door. Almost empty. This surprises me until I remind myself my mother isn't here to fill it. At the new stainless-steel sink that Mom had installed two months before she died, I find a clean glass, fill it with water, pop the pair of puffy blue Aleves in my mouth and wash them down.

The tiny crystal bear Mom hung in the window sways a little. I wonder how many times she stood in this spot, looked at the little bear and heard these same noises—the fridge humming, the TV voices, her own breathing? I try to look out the window, but all I can see is a lot of my mother in my reflection—long dark hair, narrow face.

Familiar grief pushes in and I shove it back.

After my mother passed away, my grief came in waves, like the ocean four blocks away, crashing against the cliffs. Sadness rolled over me, at times the weight of it knocking me down, filling up my throat and chest. Then just as suddenly, it would be gone, washing back to who knows where? I wouldn't know when the grief was going to splash over me again—a song, feeling the early morning breeze against my skin, anything might bring back the hurt.

I turn around, lean against the counter's edge. I grew up knowing my mother loved this kitchen. We talked a lot here. She told me once that she wanted to soak up the history of this house, and family history always began in kitchens.

She told me so many things. Once at the park, when I was around six, she held a dandelion to my lips, said, *"Make a wish, Christine, and believe!"*

I close my eyes, wish my mother were here.

"Christine," Dad calls from the living room.

"Yeah?" Where did she go? Crazy, I know, but it's so strange that one moment a person is breathing, laughing, then poof, gone!

"News is on."

"I'll be right there."

I look around the kitchen, wonder how much my father misses my mother. They were married for forty-three years. Does he plunge into memories and swim to where she is, tangle in her long, dark hair?

I drain the glass. I have to get control. I push my thoughts back and walk into the other room.

Blinking red lights grab my attention.

"What in the heck is that?" I ask.

CHAPTER 2

"What does it look like?" Dad asks.

I glance at the fake Christmas tree sitting on the table in front of the window. I don't think I should tell him the tree, leaning too far to the left, resembles a drunken sailor. He might not think that's as funny as I do. Huge red lights are looped precariously around the tree's small, fake branches, and the Santa ornaments that Mom used to place on a big, fresh tree, look like they are hanging on for dear life.

I shake my head, study a scratch in the hardwood floor.

"Something wrong?" Dad asks.

Oh, God, now he knows I don't like the tree.

"Did you put up the tree?" I ask then feel like an idiot because who else would have done it? "It's really nice," I lie.

"No it's not. It looks like crap."

"It's cute. Really."

"It's fake."

Like anyone couldn't tell! I walk to where he's sitting. He looks up, turns down the volume of the TV.

"Fake, real, it doesn't matter. I'm flattered that you put up a tree. It's a great tree."

"You never could lie very well. It's crappy. I got it at Wal-Mart, on sale. With you coming for Christmas—"

He stops, gets this weird look on his face, and the gray light from the TV accentuates his frown lines.

"What?" I turn and see my reflection in the window by the tree.

"Nothing. I thought…nothing." His expression is pure confusion. "We're missing the news." Then he points to the tree. "So you like it? The decorations are too big. If you want, we can go get a real one tomorrow."

"I wouldn't change it for the world. Really, I'm impressed. I know you don't like Christmas."

"True."

"Do you still think it's a Communist plot against

MARY SCHRAMSKI   25

democracy?" Under the tree are two badly wrapped packages. Jesus, I completely forgot to shop! "I need to go Christmas shopping."

"What?"

"I have to go Christmas shopping tomorrow." I point to the presents. "I was so busy before I left Tucson, I didn't even think of gifts."

Dad looks at me, raises an eyebrow. "How do you know they're for you?"

"Well, I…I don't."

He laughs. "They are, but they aren't much. I don't want anything. I still think it's a Communist plot. The tree seemed to need presents, that's all. You can open them now, if you want."

"No, I'll wait till—"

A commercial about Toyotas blares through the room and tramples the rest of my words. Dad turns down the volume again.

"I have to get you something. I wouldn't feel right."

"Okay. Fight the crowds to get me something I don't want or need."

I laugh at his familiar directness but feel a little hurt. I love Christmas, the presents and the fun.

"But we've always exchanged presents." An image surfaces—of my mother, a serious look on her face, wrapping boxes in pretty paper. My throat tightens and I look around the living room. The overstuffed couch, the different shades of blue in the Oriental rug that covers most of the hardwood floor, the large picture window with no curtains so early morning sunlight will rush in—all the same, and all seem to be waiting for my mother to return.

I close my eyes, want her here. Then I brush back this futile wish.

"Remember how Mom used to sing, 'I'll Be Home for Christmas' every evening, right before dinner, starting on the fifteenth?"

"Yeah, I remember." Dad stares straight ahead.

Brian Williams talks about sextuplets born yesterday in Virginia.

Dad gets up, walks over and hands me the remote. "You know, I think I'll go for a walk. Watch anything you want, honey."

"But the news isn't over." I stand, motion to Peter Jennings.

"It's all the same."

He heads toward the hallway leading to the bedrooms. I get up, follow him, stand in their bedroom doorway. The room looks the same—blue and white everywhere, a woman's room shared with her husband. Except now there are clothes piled in corners, and the bed isn't made. I can't take my eyes off the mess.

"I didn't have time to pick up," Dad says.

He's looking at me. I shrug. "Oh. So you're going for a walk now?"

"Yeah." He finds his Nikes under some clothes, sits on the edge of the bed, kicks off his loafers, then jams his feet with the black socks into tennis shoes and ties the laces in double knots.

"It's kinda late, isn't it?"

"The fresh air does me good, helps me sleep."

"But you used to run, always in the morning. You aren't doing that anymore?"

He shakes his head.

"Are you having trouble sleeping?"

He looks at me as if he's trying to think of what to say. "A little. Things have changed. I walk now, at night. It seems to help."

"Help what? The not sleeping?"

"Sometimes."

The weird feeling I have in the pit of my stomach grows. I breathe in, remind myself, yes, things change, but some things don't—like not being able to talk to your father or to feel completely relaxed around him.

"Excuse me," he says, trying to pass through the door.

"Want me to go with you?"

"Only if you want to. I stay out a long time, so if you're tired that's not such a good idea."

I step back into the hallway, knowing he wants me to stay home.

He moves past me. "Don't wait up if you're tired, honey."

A moment later I hear the back door close. In the living room the tree blinks on. I turn off the TV, go to my old room and shut the door. The white daisy bedspread I'm so used to is still on the bed. The oak dresser and highboy from Lou's Antiques in Palos Verdes stand opposite each other.

I pull back the curtain, try to look out to the front, but the window mirrors my reflection. I click off the lamp on the dresser and I disappear. Then I see my father, highlighted in the blinking red light from the fake tree. He's standing in the middle of the front yard, staring at the house.

I wonder what he's thinking. Is he happy I'm here? It sure doesn't seem like it. But he did put up the tree. Maybe he just doesn't want company. The sad part of all this is that I really don't know.

Jake McGuire looked at the house his wife Dorothy had insisted on buying thirty-eight years ago. Christine's bedroom light clicked off. He hoped his only child was going to bed. The red patch of light from the Christmas tree snapped off then on again. He crossed his arms and felt calmer than he had when he was in the house.

A few minutes ago, when he was sitting in his chair, he'd again seen an image of his wife. Jake shook his head.

Maybe all the talk about Christmas had brought it about. Then again, it could have been Christine's reflection.

No, that wasn't it.

He'd seen Dorothy standing in the middle of the living room. It was for just a split second, but he couldn't deny it.

Jake took a deep breath. Many times this past eight months, he'd wished his wife were sitting next to him or in another room. He'd even closed his eyes and pictured her standing in front of him smiling. But tonight? What he saw felt real. And seeing her made him feel comforted.

The Christmas tree lights blinked off then on, and Jake remembered why he'd bought the stupid tree. He'd gone to pick up a case of Pennz-oil on sale at Wal-Mart, and he'd heard Dorothy's favorite Christmas song, "I'll Be Home for Christmas," as he was standing in the middle of the auto supplies, for Christ's sake. That's when he realized he needed to get a tree because Christine would be home. The next thing he knew, he was shoving the artificial one in the trunk.

Jake walked away from the house, then stopped a little ways down the sidewalk. He was glad he'd come outside. He wasn't used to talking about Dorothy. Since she'd been gone, his evenings were silent, except for the TV. And he'd never been responsible for Christmas. When his wife was alive, she took care of all the holidays. Most of the time, he was flying. Lay-over hotels were quiet, and he got the best assignments for those days. Dorothy said she didn't mind, even after they got older, as long as Christine could make it home.

Deep grief invaded his body as he walked down the street. To distract himself, he looked up. The tall streetlights dabbed every fourth lawn with glassy white light. He hoped the cool night air and being out of the house, away from the memories—all the regrets—would make him feel better.

Tonight, seeing Christine for the first time since Dorothy's funeral had made him sad. She looked so much like her mother, with her dark hair, slim build and blue eyes.

Maybe all the fresh memories had made him think he saw Dorothy. Jake stopped in the middle of the street. Yeah, that was it. The same thing had happened three weeks ago, right after the evening news reported a car wreck. That's the first time he thought he saw Dorothy standing in front of him. It was for just a moment, yet he felt elated.

And later that night, loneliness covered him like a blanket, suffocating him. So he'd walked to the center of town, away from the house, the memories, the uncertainty. He stayed out for an hour, then right after he'd walked in the kitchen, Christine called, told him she'd booked a flight to come home. He'd been so depressed, he couldn't think or talk. It took him a few minutes to get it together, call her back and ask what time she was coming in.

This morning, he'd thought, with Christine home, he'd be busy and the grief would subside. Tonight, at least, he managed to talk, act normal. He certainly didn't want his daughter to worry about him.

Jake walked faster, told himself he'd keep it together while Christine was here. At Dorothy's funeral, he'd come to grips with the fact he was never going to see his wife again, despite what some people said.

You'll be together again someday.

A lot of people said that to him. He thought people spouted that bull to make themselves feel better and not so afraid of death. He believed that the spirit everlasting was pretty much crap. He stuffed his grief, held his feelings back and told himself to face reality.

Jake crossed the deserted street. There was no heaven or hell or anything in between. When he was eight, he'd announced to his mother he didn't believe in heaven. She slapped the crap out of him, and that pretty much convinced him. The woman had tried to shove her faith down his throat for years, until he joined the service and moved away from Des Moines.

He stopped at the corner. He had too much time on his hands. After Christmas, he'd paint the house, keep himself busy.

He turned west, pumped his arms, walked faster. For the first time he noticed the fog, up from the ocean and veiling everything. He thought about the pilots being vectored into LAX tonight, relying on instruments, believing in what they couldn't see, working and not thinking about anything else but getting on the ground in one piece. He envied them and wished he could still fly—look out the front left window of an airplane.

He used to love flying in the mornings. Getting up early, taking off toward the sun as it inched up the blue sky—that was his personal heaven. And he liked jogging in the mornings, too. He always got back to the house before Dorothy woke. He'd step into their cathedral-like bedroom, watch her sleep, his fingers aching to touch her dark hair streaming against her pillow.

Jake stopped at the edge of Point Fermin Park. Even though the park was only four blocks from the house, he hadn't come down here in years. The area was still thick with eucalyptus and oaks. Dorothy liked this park, and was fascinated with the abandoned lighthouse at the cliff's edge. He'd told her once she was obsessed with the lighthouse. She laughed, but he saw the hurt in her expression.

He closed his eyes—God, what a fool he'd been.

Jake took the curb too fast, staggered, then fell to his knees, palms flat against the asphalt.

"Damn!" The low grunt knifed the air.

Stunned, he got up and dusted bits of tarred gravel from his hands. He tested his legs. His knees throbbed.

Slowly he walked into the park. The last time he could remember being here was with Dorothy and Christine. Dorothy had managed to talk him into going with them. The kid was little and she romped through the thick grass. Dorothy laughed, leaned against him.

The white clapboard lighthouse tower, forty feet

away, stood between the eucalyptus trees. For the past few years, on days when the weather was good, Dorothy brought her lunch to the bench in front of the lighthouse and spent twenty minutes relaxing. At times, he'd actually been jealous of the building.

When the San Pedro City Council and the Coast Guard abandoned the place, Dorothy latched on to the hope someone would save the lighthouse. He'd told her a million times it wouldn't happen, that nobody gave a crap about a useless building and she shouldn't, either. Then he'd turned up the volume on the TV.

Jake winced, closed his eyes and wanted to go back, have one more night to listen and to talk to her. A foghorn from the Los Angeles harbor sounded, reaching out its long, thick fingers. His knees hurt and his hands burned. He needed to go home and rest. Maybe a hot shower would help him ease the pain in his knees, his chest.

He turned toward the exit to leave then stopped.

His heart began to pound. Her dark hair swayed, and the red dress with the white buttons that fitted her so well and enhanced her breasts reminded him of years ago, and how young they'd been.

Jake's throat tightened. He closed his eyes, then opened them.

But Dorothy was gone.

CHAPTER 3

I struggle out of sleep, sit up. The Christmas tree lights blink on. Dad is standing by the living room window looking out at the front yard.

"I must have fallen asleep," I say, hugging myself and leaning back on the couch where I dozed off. "I was waiting for you to come home."

Dad crosses the room, clicks on the light by his chair, goes over and pulls the plug on the tree, then looks at me. "You should go to bed."

I yawn. According to the grandfather clock in the corner, it's eleven-thirty.

"I should. How long were you out?"

"Couple of hours."

I get off the couch and notice the dirt on his pants. "What happened to your pants?"

"I fell."

"You fell? How? Are you okay?"

"Yeah. I stumbled off the curb. It's no big deal," he says, waves me away, and that's when I see the blood on his hand.

"Dad, your hand is bleeding!" I go to him, take his wrist gingerly and try to look at his palm.

"It's nothing." He pulls away, walks through the dining room to the kitchen. I find him at the sink, filling a glass with water.

"You sure you're okay?"

He nods, drinks. Water drips on the front of his chambray shirt, tiny dark tear shapes. I begin to feel light-headed. He turns back around, rinses his palms and grimaces.

"You should put something on your hand." I look at his pants again. There isn't any blood and I'm thankful for that. "You sure your knees are okay?"

"There's Neosporin somewhere around here. When I find it, I'll put some on."

Dad walks back to the living room and I tag along. He sits, groans, then looks at me and forces a smile. "I'm fine."

"I know where the Neosporin is." And for one deep, long moment, I want my mother to be here so badly I can't breathe. I shake the thought away, go to the medicine cabinet, locate the ointment and come back to the living room.

"Here, put your hand out." He does, and I dab the antibiotic on the small oozing areas.

"The other one is scraped, too." He holds his left hand out.

It's not as bad as his right one, thank God. "This must have taken the fun out of your walk," I say, trying to be funny as I dab on more ointment.

He gives me this weird look, for just a moment—a split second really—and then it's gone. But it's too late and I'm more worried than I was before.

"Maybe you should go to the doctor to check—"

"I'm not going to the doctor."

"What if you broke something?"

"I'm okay. I've had broken bones before and I know what that feels like."

"Where'd you fall?" I ask as I put the cap on the Neosporin.

"On my knees."

"No, I mean where were you?"

"Over by the park."

"Oh, you walked to the park?"

"Yeah."

"I haven't been there in years. Is it the same?"

Instead of answering, he closes his eyes. And I notice how pale his skin looks, pallid really. And the wrinkles on his forehead are much deeper than I remember.

"Dad?"

He looks at me. "Yeah?"

"Can I get you something? Maybe some hot chocolate or anything, another glass of water?"

"Hot chocolate would be good." He pushes himself up with his elbows, his hands held high.

"I'll make it," I say, and we go into the kitchen. A few moments later, the hot chocolate sizzles in the pan. I stand at the stove, not knowing what to do. Dad is by the sink. I smile at him.

"I did the dishes." I nod toward the sink.

"Thanks. Kitchen looks nice."

"Is it cold outside?"

"A little."

The house is so quiet and colorless without my mother. "The house seems kind of lonely."

"It is."

"How are you doing really?"

"Every day is tough...but I'm okay." He purses his lips, shakes his head like a kid, and I feel so sorry for him.

I study the table for a moment, try to think of something that might make him feel better. When I look back, he's staring at me. "Someone told me it gets easier."

"That *someone* lied." Dad straightens a little, looks at the pan on the stove. "Chocolate ready?"

"I think so." I look for mugs that don't remind me of my mother, but it's impossible. I finally give up, fill two bright yellow ones that are as familiar as my own reflection.

"It's hot, so be careful with your hands." I place the steaming mugs on the oak table.

We sit across from each other. "So you walked around the park? Isn't it kind of dark there at night?"

"Yeah."

"I've never been there at night."

He looks down, gingerly brings the mug to his lips, blows across the surface. "What do you want to do tomorrow?"

"Well, you know I need to go Christmas shopping. We could go to the mall early before it gets busy. I'll buy you lunch after."

"Still gonna challenge the crowds?"

I nod. "You could come with me, if you feel okay. I'll drive. We don't have to stay out long."

"No thanks."

I fill my lungs. "Doing something with a friend?"

"Nah. Thought I'd hang out around the house, get some work done."

"Do you see any of your friends?"

"Chet and I have a beer once in a while. Most of our friends were your mother's. She was good at making friends."

Chet is a friend of my father's. They knew each other in Vietnam. He's a nice guy, quiet, tall and gray-haired like my father.

"I know, but they liked you, too. You could still go to dinner with them, have a drink. It's got to be lonely without people around," I say, knowing this from experience. I don't have a lot of friends in Tucson because I work too much. When I'm home, I watch TV, then fall into bed so I can start another day early.

"People quit calling months ago."

I think back to the time of the funeral. The phone rang and rang and rang, and for the two days I was home the house was thick with people. Now the house is almost silent.

"What do you do all day?" It's funny how I've known my father all my life, but I don't *really* know him. It was always my mother who made the plans, talked to people. She was the life in this house.

"I watch TV, walk, putter around. This spring I'm going to paint. Your mother always wanted me to paint the house yellow."

A memory presses in, takes center stage. My mother standing by the kitchen sink, telling me she met my father on a beach at sunrise when the sun looked like a big pat of *butter*. I can almost hear her voice, the way she said the word. Even then I thought it odd, yet so much like her. She held out her arms, danced me around the room, and I laughed when she told me I'd find my Prince Charming, and we'd have a soft yellow house.

A sigh escapes my lips.

"What?"

I shake my head. "Nothing. We've had enough happen tonight."

"You said something."

"No, I sighed. I was thinking about when Mom told me she met you at Cabrillo Beach at sunrise when the sun looked like *butter*. You know how she used to talk, and how she loved the color yellow." My words cut the air like typewriter keys. "How she always said I'd find the right guy."

His lips flatten a little. "We met on Cabrillo Beach in the morning. It might have been sunny." His solemn expression crumbles a little, and I feel his sorrow under my heart, beneath my eyes.

"You know, when I was about six, she told me the sun spilled out a big puddle of lemonade when it was sunny."

Dad takes another sip of hot chocolate, clears his throat. "I'd better go to bed. Thanks for the hot chocolate. " He scoots his chair back.

I watch him rinse his mug, rub his fingers around the edge, then put it upside down in the sink. He walks out of the room, and I swear, for a moment, I can feel my mother's arms around me.

* * *

It's early morning and I'm standing on the sidewalk that edges Point Fermin Park. The area almost matches the memory I tucked away years ago, except the park looks smaller, not as bright. Every time I come home I have this same experience—things look different, not by much, but enough to startle me for a moment.

The wet grass paints the bottom of my jeans as I walk across it. I woke at seven, found Dad sitting at the kitchen table sipping coffee from the same mug he used last night. He was working the *New York Times* crossword puzzle, like he always does. I checked his hands. They looked much better, scabbed over and not so red. He seemed okay, told me he's fine and I should have a great walk.

The sky is California blue, clear. I walk past the old bench, reach the lookout point and wrap my fingers around the metal railing. Cold slips to my fingers, moves up my arms and finds my shoulders. The ocean below rolls back and forth, like a window shade, rhythmically drenching the rocks.

To the right, the abandoned lighthouse sits. My mother once told me she loved the lighthouse because it brought people home. When she'd say things like that, I'd laugh and tell her it was ridiculous to *love* an old building.

The ocean breeze lifts strands of my hair, dances them around my face. I make a stab at brushing them back, then give up and study the lighthouse again, remember my mother explaining years ago that it was built in the 1800s. Two women ran it until they got so lonely they moved back to Los Angeles and both found true love. I told her I didn't care.

Oh, honey, you need to let yourself dream.

A wave of hurt rushes into my chest, fills up my lungs. Maybe coming to the park wasn't such a good idea. I turn, cut across the length of grass, take the sidewalk to the Point Fermin Café and go inside.

People are scattered throughout the familiar restaurant, sitting at wooden tables or large booths. "Have Yourself a Merry Little Christmas" meanders from the radio on the freezer and floats through the braided conversations.

I order coffee and smile at the young waitress because she's sweet, so young she looks like a colt, and it isn't her fault my mother isn't here. As she heads toward the kitchen, a man walks by, stops, turns around.

"Christine McGuire?"

"Yes," I say, before I realize I don't know him. He smiles as if I should. Out of habit, I stand when he offers his hand.

"Don't get up."

"Do I know you?" I ask. I squint, really look at him.

"Well, you used to. We went to high school together."

High school, my God. His face looks a little familiar, but I can't remember his name. I was a nobody in high school, like ninety percent of the kids, and I hated it.

"Adam Williams," he says, like he knows I don't remember him.

"Right. How are you? It's been a long time." Short dark hair covers his head. He's an average-looking man. I have the same sensation I did in the park, where things look kind of the same, but not really.

"Yeah, twenty some years." He laughs and I

laugh, a reaction like a yawn that people sometimes share. "I don't know why I expected you to
recognize me."

And then, for a moment, I'm seventeen, in a
stuffy classroom, sitting across from Adam. I smile,
feel like a teenager. "Oh, yeah, now I remember
you."

Johnny Mathis begins singing "Walking in a
Winter Wonderland" and someone turns up the radio.

"Christmas music. God, I've had enough already," I say.

"What?"

"The Christmas music." I gesture toward the radio on the freezer.

He looks confused, then laughs. "I love Christmas
music, always have. They should play it all year."

"Please, no. I loved it before they started playing it in October." This isn't exactly the truth. I
loved it until my mother died, but why go into this
with someone I hardly know?

He motions to the chair across from the one I
just got out of. "Mind if I join you for a minute?
Catch up on old times."

"Well, I guess not." I don't really want to talk or even think, but what can I say? I didn't sleep well last night, when I finally got to bed, and then I woke up early.

The young waitress comes by. Adam shakes his head when she asks him if he wants anything.

"So," he says, hesitates.

I take a sip of coffee. I know how he feels. It's like we've been sitting next to each other on a long plane trip; there's a faint connection, but nothing really.

"I never thought I'd see you again," I say lamely to fill up the silent space.

"Why's that?"

"Well…I guess, I don't know really. I just thought that."

"You still live in San Pedro?"

"No. Tucson. I'm here for the week, for Christmas." I gesture toward the peeling Christmas lights surrounding the old wooden window.

"I moved back to Pedro seven years ago." He leans forward a little. "I love it here."

"Back from where?" I try not to stare at him, but it's utterly impossible. One moment, he looks like someone I remember, and then the next like a man my age, but someone I don't even know.

Adam glances out the window, then back to me. "I lived all over. Before I came home, I moved around a lot. Never thought I'd miss this town, but I did as I got older."

"Why's that?" I ask, yet I understand. The last few years, I've missed San Pedro, too.

"I like the ocean, the small-town atmosphere. When I came back, it wasn't exactly what I remembered, but close."

"I just had that same experience over at the park." The image of my dad falling off the curb by the park last night pops into my mind, and I shake my head.

"Something wrong?"

"No...yes. My dad isn't exactly the same, either."

"People change, too. First rule of Zen Buddhism, things change, and to negate misery we have to accept those changes." He closes his eyes as if he's praying, then opens them and stares at me.

"Really?" Now I remember. Adam was the *weird* smart guy in high school.

He shrugs, grins a little. "Yeah, well, something like that. I've read some books on Buddhism. It fascinates me. What kind of work do you do?"

"Realtor."

"Great. I'm an electrical engineer." Adam laughs. "I think everyone in high school thought I'd end up a bum."

I laugh, too. "No. Maybe a professor, or a rocket scientist. You were so smart. But we really didn't know each other."

"You were the shy, pretty one."

"High school was a long time ago."

"Did you know I quit high school?" he asks.

"You did?"

He nods, grins again.

"As boring as it was, I wondered why I stayed."

"Actually, I got thrown out." He leans back, rests his right arm over the vacant chair beside him. "I think it had something to do with the principal getting tired of me harassing teachers about what they didn't know. After that I worked graveyard shift at the Pacific Street 7-Eleven for three weeks."

"Only three weeks?"

He leans forward again. "Yeah. One night, right

before Christmas, a woman came in and right behind her two guys. The woman needed Tampax, the guys dope. They robbed us both."

"Jesus," I whisper.

"Yeah, that's just what I was thinking, when the taller of the two put his Smith & Wesson to my head."

"Thank God you weren't killed."

"That was my second thought. It changed me. Decided to go back to school. Plus, it made me realize I wanted to live, do something with my life to make a difference."

"So are you doing that?"

"Every day I try to help someone."

"That's nice."

"Sometimes it's difficult to find a person who needs help."

"It is?"

"It is. You'd be surprised."

"So when did you go back to school?"

"I punched a cash register for eight hours, but that wasn't very interesting, and I was a rebel without a clue. Maybe I still am."

I laugh. "And then what happened?"

"I financed a beat-up Harley at sixteen percent, rode around the country doing a bad imitation of *Easy Rider,* ran out of money in central Oregon, went to work in another 7-Eleven, was robbed again, then got my GED and went to college. I was a slow learner."

I think about how I had to learn so many lessons the hard way. About jobs, men and life in general. "At least you learned. So you're an electrical engineer?"

"Yeah. It's the greatest job in the world. Good money, honest work. As long as I don't electrocute myself I'm happy." He points toward the window, the Christmas lights, and bounces in his seat. "I bring artificial sunshine to the world."

"Right," I say, feeling my eyes get a little bigger. Adam is so animated.

"How about you? How are you changing the world?" He leans toward me, smiles.

I sit back, think about telling him I sell people their dreams. "I sell real estate. I enjoy it and I've done pretty well. It keeps me busy."

He laughs. "Good for you. You sell people places to be happy."

"Maybe. After they sign the contract, it's up to them."

"So your family's still here?"

"Yes…well, my dad." And for the first time this morning, I realize that's all the family I have.

"Married?"

"No. Never."

"Is that, No you never have married or you never will?"

I laugh at his slight insanity. "It's I've never been married and since I'm going on forty-three, it's not very likely."

"Anything's possible. Remember that." He leans his head back a little. "Life is all about believing." He looks around the room, then back to me. "I hardly ever come in here, but this morning I had this weird feeling, like I needed to be here."

And for a moment, I'm back in a high school classroom with its chalky haze, and Adam is sitting, slouched in his chair, his eyes half closed, giving the teacher a bunch of crap.

CHAPTER 4

I'm standing on the porch, looking through the living room window. My father is sitting in his chair, holding my mother's picture, and his expression is so despondent, it hurts to look at him.

My plan, after I left the café, was to come home, borrow Dad's car and go Christmas shopping. But then, a moment ago, as I was crossing the porch, I noticed Dad through the living room window.

He glances up, sees me. I smile and give him a little wave. He walks over to the fireplace and puts her picture back on the mantel.

"How was your walk?" he asks, coming out onto the porch.

"Okay, until I went to the park. It reminded me of Mom, so I left and went over to the café and drank too much coffee."

He doesn't say anything, just looks at me. Were

our conversations always this stilted or did I just never notice when Mom was around?

"Maybe it was seeing the lighthouse, too, not just the park," I say. "You know how Mom loved the…" The anguish in his eyes stops the rest of what I was going to say. I want to tell him that everything—the house with all of her things still out, the park, even the air—reminds me of her. But I don't. He looks like he's hurting, plus we don't have the kind of relationship where I can bare my soul.

"Hey, I ran into someone I knew in high school at the café. We talked a little."

"That's good." Dad looks out past the front porch to the lawn.

"You were holding Mom's picture?" I gesture toward the window.

His gaze comes back to me. "Yeah, I've been thinking about her a lot."

"I have, too."

He rubs his lips. "Her two big things in December were trying to get you to come home and putting me in the Christmas spirit."

My heart pounds. I cross the porch, place my

hand on his forearm. "Mom knew us pretty well. Sometimes I had to work, so did you. You two were together a long time. She understood."

"At times…"

I wait for him to finish, then realize he's not going to.

"At times?" I urge, then pat his arm, feel the warmth under his shirt.

He shakes his head. "Nothing."

"Dad, Mom…" It feels good talking to someone who knew my mother, who loved her. I miss that in Tucson. Yet the way my father looks, I think this talk might upset him.

"Your mother what?" he asks.

"She wouldn't want you to be sad. She wasn't like that. Maybe you should think about the good times. That's what I try to do." This isn't true. My memories come at will, dodge in and out, like sunlight in between the trees on a windy day.

"It's not that easy. I keep thinking there are things I should have done."

"I know. Me, too."

He looks at me, squints. "What do you know?"

"Mom called me the night before her accident,

and I didn't call her back. How...stupid was that? I regret that."

"She always called you. Worried when you didn't call back. You should have been more responsible when it came to your mother."

"I know," I say, and my chest starts to ache.

He turns, studies the yard again, and I wish our lives were the way they used to be—my mother standing between us, keeping my father and me apart.

"She wanted you to go to college, get a good education," he says quietly.

I think about how my mother used to send me money when I was job-hopping, little notes about how I should go out and buy something fun. She probably never told Dad.

I walk to where he can see me. "No, that was *you* who wanted that. And I think I've done pretty well for myself. It just took some time."

"I wanted you to be something."

I try not to feel angry, but it's impossible with old hurts surfacing. "I *am* something! At least Mom thought so."

I wait for an answer, but his eyes hold so much

loneliness I have to look away. Before I can say another word, he goes inside.

"Hi," Sandra says. "I was hoping you'd come by."
She leans against the front doorjamb and smiles.
"It's good to see you."

I'm standing on Sandra's porch. She looks the
same—long red hair, creamy skin, sweet expression.

"Good to see you, too," I say.

"You look great." Her smile widens.

"Thanks, so do you."

"Oh, I do *not*. I'm as big as a horse, but I don't
care." She pats her stomach and laughs. "I've been
on every diet known to womankind and none of
them work. I've just decided I'm going to be fat."

"You aren't fat."

"Right, now if you add *You're just a big-boned girl*,
you'll sound just like your mother."

She laughs again and I start to, but something
happens inside me. I look down, study the porch
floor, feel like I'm going to start crying, but I manage to swallow back the tears, look up and smile.

"Tine, are you okay?"

"Yeah, I'm fine."

"Well, come inside. It's been so long since you've even been over to the house. Get in here." Sandra draws me into the house, and we stand in the middle of her parents' familiar living room. More nostalgic feelings rush through me. The house is the same, homey as ever. Sandra's mother, Josephine, loved antiques, deep burgundies and dark wood, the opposite of my mother's taste, yet just as pretty.

"Are you having a nice visit?"

"I am," I say, still feeling like an idiot for almost breaking down in front of her. I certainly don't need to lay my problems on her. She has enough of her own.

"I'm glad. I can't believe it's almost Christmas. Where has the time gone? Let's go into the kitchen."

We walk in the kitchen, and Sandra extends her hand as if presenting a grand prize on a game show. "Still the same old place. I haven't changed much, haven't had time. Sit right here." She pats the 1940s café booth her parents found in an alley behind a restaurant years ago. "You want a drink?"

I laugh. "It's not even *two*."

"So? It's 5:00 p.m. somewhere. Let's have a drink to celebrate you being home and actually coming over to see me."

"I don't think I can handle a drink right now. Too early."

"How about some hot chocolate?"

"Sure." When we were little, Sandra's mother used to let us practice our cooking skills on Saturday afternoons in her crazy warm kitchen. When Sandra's grandfather passed away, we made a gloppy mess of chocolate syrup, milk and maraschino cherries for Josephine, brought it to her while she was sitting on the couch looking out the window. She smiled, hugged us both. That was the day she taught us to make hot chocolate from scratch.

"I still make it like Mama did." Sandra turns from the stove, milk in hand. "Remember?"

"Of course. How could I forget that?"

"You look great. I swear you never change."

"Oh, God, I look like hell. Last week I worked fourteen-hour days so I could come home for the holidays, so I'm worn out."

"That's a lot of hours. You must really like your job."

"Oh, yeah. Love it. I'm the top-selling Realtor in my office."

"I'm the top receptionist in my office, but I'm the only one so it was easy to be first." She smiles wider. Sandra is big in every way. Always has been. She is three inches taller than I am. Even her hair is big—curly red, four inches past her shoulders and wild.

She turns the heat under the milk down low. "Do you really want hot chocolate or were you just being nice?"

I shake my head. "I've had about a million cups of coffee this morning."

"Then you certainly don't need any more liquid." She snaps off the burner, takes the saucepan and shoves it in the refrigerator. "We'll have it later."

She walks over to the booth that is wedged in the bay window and sits across from me. "Since I've moved back home, I can't tell you how many times I've thought of you. Just the other night I was thinking about how we used truth serum to tell all our secrets. Remember that?"

"How could I forget?" I laugh. She was sixteen-and-a-half. I was thirteen. Friday nights were truth-serum nights if Sandra didn't have a date. We'd pour Coke in a juice glass, add five teaspoons of sugar, drink it down in one gulp. And then we'd laugh our butts off, probably from the sugar high.

She'd tell me secrets about the kids she went to school with, the boy she might be dating.

"Remember what you told your mother one time about Tommy Bradford?"

I shake my head, try to remember, then suddenly the memory comes pouring in. I told my mother Sandra let her boyfriend touch her breasts.

"Will you ever forgive me?"

"No." She shakes her head. "My mother wouldn't let me date him again."

"Whatever happened to him?"

"Tommy's selling shoes at the Del Amo Shopping Center. Been married and divorced three times, has four kids, and last I heard, but this is from a not reputable source—read, Tiffany Brown—he was living at the Torrance YMCA."

"Maybe I did you a favor."

"Oh, yeah, thanks. My mother put me on restriction for a month. You know how long a month is to a sixteen-year-old?"

My mother was tucking me in bed. I was a late developer and she was explaining that soon I'd need a training bra. I whispered that Sandra's boyfriend touched her titties. Her blue eyes widened, but she didn't say a word.

"Okay, speaking of dating, are you? I promise I won't tell Jake any of the details." Sandra grins.

"No. I don't date, I work. And Dad doesn't seem to care what I do. We had a small blowout on the front porch a little while ago." This slips out, and I shake my head.

"About what?"

"I'm not sure how it started, but it got around to how he wanted me to go to college years ago. I got angry."

"Oh, that's just him." She waves her hand toward our house. "He was always that way."

"True, but it doesn't make it any easier."

"Did you end on an okay note?"

"He walked into the house, and I walked over here. Do you mind if we talk about something else?" I don't want to think about my father's sad face, or the anger I couldn't hold back.

"Of course not. So you aren't dating anyone?"

"I haven't had a date in probably a year. I'm too busy. How about you?"

"How are you defining a date?" She grins.

"Drinks, maybe dinner," I say.

"Not a date, not a meeting, not even an intimate handshake. Who's in this town to date?"

We both laugh and, for a moment, I feel like years ago, when we'd sit in the kitchen and talk for hours.

"That reminds me. Guess who I saw at the café?"

"What is this, twenty questions? Who'd you see?"

"Adam Williams."

Sandra stares at me. "Who the hell is Adam Williams?"

I laugh again, feel good. "I went to school with him. So did you. Don't you remember? He was the guy who used to walk around the school with a calculator doing square roots."

"Brown hair, tall, average looking, pimples?"

"Yeah the brown hair, but no pimples."

"They all looked like that."

"He always gave teachers crap about what they didn't know. Really smart."

"Yeah, and?"

"I walked over to the café this morning, and he

was there. He's an engineer. Still different, very nice, though."

"And why did you walk over to the Lard Yard early this morning?"

"Oh, I needed fresh air, some exercise."

"Don't we all." She looks out the window.

I close my eyes for a moment, to get centered, tell myself to quit thinking about missing my mother. Then I look at Sandra.

"Is your dad okay otherwise? I don't see him much."

"He seems lonely. He hasn't changed a thing in the house, except it's a mess and he's walking at night, which I think is weird."

"Hey, walking is good for the heart," Sandra says. "You know when my dad died, my mother got a little…" She stops. "Oh, hell, let's not talk about this stuff. It's too depressing."

"Okay."

"Just remember, it takes a long time to get over a death. Jake's probably still dealing with a lot."

"Probably," I say, knowing this is true. "I just thought I'd come home and we'd connect because Mom is gone. You know, there wouldn't be friction."

"Maybe you need to give it more time."

"We've had forty-some years. And I didn't realize how coming back was going to affect me. I miss my mother a lot."

"I miss her, too. Remember how she used to put on her makeup just so?" Sandra brings her hands to her face, strokes the sides.

And for a moment, I fall into a memory. My mother sitting at her vanity, looking back and smiling at me.

"It took me two years to feel okay after my father passed away, and I wasn't as close to him as you were to your mother. Hospice says it takes time."

"Are you still working there?"

She nods. "I'll be there forever. I guess it's my way of making the world a little better. They don't pay me enough, but I stay. And the office is up on Western, close to Mama."

"How's she doing?" I ask.

"She's hanging in there. The nursing home is nice, well, as nice as it can be. But every day when I go into her room, I feel guilty. But I remind myself I have to work."

"It wouldn't be safe for her to be alone." I try to

reassure her, but I'm not sure how. What does it feel like to be responsible for your parent?

Sandra nods, smiles a little. "You know, when I made the final decision to put her in the nursing home, I found her five blocks away, standing in the middle of the street, and she didn't know where she was." She sighs, rubs her eyes.

I think about Josephine, how I loved her. She was always so concerned, warm.

"What?" Sandra asks.

"I was just thinking about your mom."

"Yeah, I do that a lot." Sandra gets up and looks out the window to the backyard. "I see your dad once in a while, working around the house. He seems okay. Sad, distracted, but I guess that's to be expected. I mean, anyone who knew your parents knew how crazy he was about your mother. And to have it happen so fast, not be able to say good-bye…" She stops, turns back to me. "I'm sorry."

"No, it's okay." I take a deep breath. "I'm doing okay. You know years ago, did you think we'd be sitting here talking about this?"

"No." Sandra walks back, taps the table, smiles. "How many boys did we moon over at this booth?"

"I miss those times. First, boys, then worrying about parents. What's next? Our own aches and pains?"

"Oh, God. You know what we need?"

"A second-base date?" I say, laugh, and she does, too.

"Well, yeah that, too. It's almost Christmas, how about a little brandy? Oh, God you're going to think I'm an alcoholic. I'm not really. Just so happy you're here. It's nice to see you again."

One time, when Sandra came home from college, I'd just graduated from high school. She bought two bottles of champagne to celebrate for just the two of us. Her parents were gone for the weekend. We got drunk and passed out on the living room floor. My mother found us the next morning throwing up.

"Do you remember the champagne episode?" I ask.

"How could I forget? I still can't drink champagne."

I hold up my hand, like I'm making a toast. "Hey, to second-base dates and brandy before five."

Sandra goes to the cabinet where Josephine always kept the liquor. "I'm glad we ditched the hot chocolate idea. Brandy is a much better drink."

Jake crossed the dark porch and went down the steps. A moment ago, he felt like he was going to explode if he didn't get out of the house.

He walked down the street. When he got to the edge of Point Fermin Park, he stopped and studied the sky.

The stars looked close, bright. Visibility had to be at least fifty miles tonight. Dorothy had read him a poem on a night just like this.

Jake sat on the hard curb and tried to remember more of that evening, hoping none of the details had faded.

That night, they had taken a walk, and when they'd gotten back to the house, Dorothy had come into their bedroom holding a thick book. She'd placed it on the nightstand, carefully took off all her clothes and lay next to him.

A moment later, she picked up the book and turned to a marked page. Her voice was soft, smooth, as always.

"And as silently…" Jake whispered the few poetic words he could remember.

Anguish and hurt gripped his body. The poetry book was still in the house. He hadn't given anything away because he couldn't bring himself to do that. He'd find the poem, read it aloud, and maybe more of the memory would return.

Jake fought his tears by turning his face up to the night sky. Looking for a poem his dead wife read to him wasn't going to do any good. He needed to accept that memories would eventually fade.

But that night, when she lay beside him, naked except for the white sheet, he hadn't paid much attention to her poem. Even at his age, all he could think about was her naked body close to his.

Even when he outlined her hip with his hand, Dorothy continued reading. When she finished the poem, she asked if he liked it. Before he could answer, she drew two circles on the inside of his elbow with her index finger.

Hey, she'd said. Then pulled the sheet up to her chin, made him promise to listen.

He'd groaned. Dorothy was always trying to make him into something he wasn't, but she was naked, and it was a nice evening, with cool air coming in from the open window, so he agreed.

She told him to close his eyes and let the poetic words take him away. Her voice was so nice, smooth, and as she read, he'd thought of tents and Arabs.

"And the night shall be filled with music and the cares…" Jake whispered, then rubbed his face. Her touch, her breath, all evaporated.

He began sobbing. Big gusts of emotional pain ripped through his body and poured out into the air. He doubled over, moaned and cried harder as saliva dripped from his mouth.

Minutes later, Jake was dry, spent from hard grief. He rubbed his eyes, then told himself he had to get control. Christine was here, and she didn't need to see him like this. Today, he'd seen the anguish on her face, the grief in her eyes. *The poor kid*. She'd been close to Dorothy.

Jake stood, walked fast into the park, pumping his arms. He breathed hard through his mouth because his nose was full from crying. He wanted to get over this grief. He'd always been able to compartmentalize his feelings, and that's what he needed to do now. He stopped, stared straight ahead.

The lighthouse stood in between the trees, white wood playing hide-and-seek between the eucalyptus and oaks. The ocean waves far below washed the park with sound and mirrored his heartbeat.

Dorothy liked it here, even in December. When she asked him to walk with her to the park, jokingly he told her going to the park would take away his Christmas spirit—he was used to Des Moines snow. She laughed, claimed nothing could put Jake McGuire in a Christmas mood. Yet, he noticed the hurt on her face as she tuned the radio to a station playing holiday music and continued decorating.

But he and Dorothy never held any pretenses between them. From the very beginning, they didn't really match, no matter how Dorothy tried to change him.

They'd met on Cabrillo Beach one summer morning. He was stationed at Point Mugu, fighting his way through pilot training. He'd come down the coast to get his head on straight. She was sitting on a yellow towel facing the ocean. Frustrated, he'd walked to the water's edge, picked up a shell and pitched it at a wave. And she'd yelled, *Hey, don't throw my seashells away.*

When he looked back, she stood. Her legs were long and tanned, her red shorts and white shirt fitting her body nicely. Suddenly, she was standing beside him, handing him a shell.

They'd gone out only two times when she confessed she loved him. Her words stunned him. He told her he wasn't sure he could love anyone. He didn't tell her then that he felt cold inside.

After his statement about love, she smiled, said that certainly wasn't true, she could feel the love in Jake McGuire. He laughed and told her not to get hung up on him. A month later, he was sent to Nam. She wrote him every day, telling him she was praying and hoping for him. He wrote back that he was glad because he couldn't do it for himself.

Jake stood by the park bench and looked around. Dorothy had spent a lot of time here. And now, being here made him feel closer to her. His chest relaxed a little.

He looked at the lighthouse again, took the dirt path around the building, pushed through the broken-down gate. At the door, Jake noticed a paper tacked to the wood. He leaned closer, read the large print. The city was going to tear down the lighthouse in a month. He yanked on the padlock, but it stood its ground.

Jake made his way around to the cliffs. The air was filled with the ocean, and it blew against his skin. He grabbed the lookout-point railing. Below he could see the white foam from the waves.

How could they rip down the building she loved? Where would he come after it was gone? He didn't want anything else to change.

His stomach tied into a hard knot and he swallowed. Grief rolled through him, banged against every muscle, made him ache. If these feelings continued, after Christmas, after Christine went home, maybe he'd come here…

Jake's heart raced and his eyes teared. There were times he didn't think he could go on feeling like this. A tiny sound startled him, and he whirled around, stumbled forward. The dark lighthouse outlined itself against the sky.

"*Hey.*"

"What?" he said out of habit. He swung back around. His head began to throb and his chest felt as if it was on fire. He had the urge to run until he was home, but he couldn't move.

There was Dorothy in her red dress, her hair swaying. And just as suddenly she disappeared.

CHAPTER 5

Jake sat on the park bench. He was confused as hell. Had he actually heard Dorothy's voice?

That was impossible, he knew, but why did he feel as if he'd seen and heard her? And for that one split second Dorothy looked and sounded so real. The same feeling, a happiness he couldn't describe, had rushed through him. The same feeling he had when they were first married and he came home from a trip to their cheap apartment. His heart beat faster and his chest felt as if it were going to explode with happiness.

He took a deep breath, stood and looked at the night sky. There was no way he could deny what he'd seen and heard.

It's ten-thirty at night, and I'm waiting for my father to come home. I look down at my pajamas and brush the toast crumbs from them. I didn't have anything to do, so I made myself some toast. I'm wearing red-and-green pj's, the ones my mother sent me for Christmas last year, when I was too busy to come home.

About an hour ago, I went to bed, then I thought I heard the front door open, then close. I got up to check it out and that's when I realized Dad wasn't home.

I peek out the back door, walk down the steps, then around the house to see if I can find him. My feet are bare and the dew wets my skin. I hug myself. I should have put on shoes. I head back inside and shiver, wish he'd stay home so I wouldn't have to worry about him.

When I first got up, I turned on the radio so I wouldn't have to listen to the house creak and my own breathing. But now I can't handle one more Christmas song and I snap off Bing Crosby as he's singing *if only in my dreams*. But I remember my mom loved that song, so I turn the radio back on and music fills the room again.

The back door opens and Dad walks in right after *please have snow and mistletoe*. He's wearing the same clothes he's had on for the past two days, his chambray shirt and khakis. I sniff, smell a mixture of BO and ocean. Oh, God.

"Were you walking?" I ask. My heart begins to slam with worry. "I thought you said you were going to bed."

He looks at me, his mouth half-open. He sighs as if I'm the last thing he needs to see, crosses the kitchen and pushes through the swinging door. I follow, expect to find him in the living room, sitting in his chair, but he's not there.

The Christmas tree lights blink at me. It's been a long day and I'm not in the Christmas mood, so I walk over, yank the plug out and head down the hallway.

"Dad?"

He's sitting on the bed, shuffling through a stack of files. He looks up, then returns to his shuffling.

"Dad?"

"Yeah?"

I sit beside him. He really stinks. How long has it been since he's had a shower? My father has always been such a neat person.

"Where did you go?" I ask, feeling weird sitting here on the bed next to him.

"I took a walk...to the park. I needed some fresh air."

"You could have opened a window." I point to the bedroom window. "I fell asleep, woke up because I heard a noise and found you were gone. I was worried."

He smiles weakly. "I didn't mean to wake you up. I'm fine. Just couldn't sleep." He thumbs through more folders.

I touch his shoulder. "What are you looking for? Maybe I can help."

"Some papers."

I sigh, feel like I'm playing "Who's on First," a game Mom and I used to have fun with when I was a kid.

"Dad."

He glances up, sighs. "I'm trying to find my retirement folders. I'm going to do something."

"You look tired." I glance at the folders, see the retirement one on his lap at the bottom. "Is that the one you're looking for?"

"Yeah, thanks." He pulls it out, puts it to the side.

"Are you sure you're all right?"

"I'm fine."

"Why do you need these so late? Are you worried about something?"

"I want to do something for your mother."

"What?"

He shakes his head. "I'll tell you about it when I get back from the bank in the morning. That way I'll know I can really make it work."

"Why are you going to the bank?" I follow him to the closet, kneel down next to him as if we're praying. My mother's brown Bass loafers are still sitting on the floor next to his black dress shoes, and this startles me a little. Her shoes...just waiting, as if she went to the store for milk. I swallow, close my eyes to get my balance.

Dad pulls out more files, looks at the tabs, then tosses each one in a small heap on the floor next to a pile of his clothes. Finally, he finds the one he needs.

"You seem so agitated."

"I'm fine." He gets up. "Yep, this is all of it. Tomorrow morning, first thing, I'll go to the bank."

"But why?"

"I'll explain after, when I know it's going to work. You said I needed something to do. After I'm finished tomorrow, you can use the car to go Christmas shopping."

"I don't understand all this." That's all I have energy to say. I stand, go to the doorway, turn around and look at him. He hasn't shaved and his hair is messy. "Dad, I think you need a shower," I say, then wish I hadn't. I don't want to hurt his feelings.

He blinks. "What?"

"You kinda smell bad," I say gently. "And I'll go with you in the morn—"

"Thanks, but I want to do this alone."

"We could get breakfast."

"I'll go, then when I come back, you can go shopping."

I nod, feel my stomach tighten and I head back to my room. I close the door, turn off the light and lean against it. My chest is aching with hurt.

"Shit," I whisper, then walk across the room and climb into bed.

I've been up since five. I didn't sleep well. Dad and I are sitting in the living room. The 7:00 a.m.

sunshine washes through the window, making the Christmas tree look more fake than ever. He's holding a pad with a full page of writing. His hair still isn't combed and there are bags under his eyes. Obviously, he didn't get much sleep, either.

"But, Dad, the bank doesn't open till nine. Why would you go down there this early?" I ask, hearing the tired whine in my voice.

"I've got to go to City Hall first." He waves the pad of paper he's holding at me. "They have to listen to me. They open at eight. I want to be the first one there."

"They have to listen to you about *what?*"

"I'm going to do something for your mother."

"I know, you told me that last night. What is it?"

"I'll explain when I come back, when I know everything is set." He looks down, brushes at his dirty khakis, then gets up and goes into the kitchen.

"Wait." I get off the couch, catch up to him. I want him to talk to me, explain what the hell he's doing. "Have another cup of coffee and we'll talk."

"Okay."

"Okay?" I look at him, surprised that he agreed.

"Yeah, you make more coffee."

I turn toward the coffeepot, feel relieved that I changed his mind. "You know, Dad, you've been acting a little dif—"

"I think I'll head on down to City Hall. I can wait outside." I hear the back door open, close.

I sprint across the kitchen, out the door, stub my toe on the last porch step. "Shit! Wait," I yell.

"You okay?" His hand is on the garage doorknob.

I squeeze my eyes against the pain. "Yeah, I'm freaking fine. I just jammed my toe back to my heel, but don't worry about me."

"I'll be back in a while." He waves, but it's more like a wave-off.

The garage swallows him. A moment later, the Volvo rumbles, the larger door lifts with a huge groan, and he backs the car out. He sees me, smiles weakly, and I'm positive some alien has taken over my father's body.

I've just hung up the phone. After Dad left, I limped into the house, sat in a kitchen chair with my foot propped up and a Ziploc bag full of ice on my toe. I've been trying to sort out why he's acting so weird, which of course isn't easy since he never told me what he's planning to do. I have the feeling that it has a lot to do with my mother's death.

Every fifteen minutes or so, I hobbled to the back door to check to see if he might have come to his senses and driven home, but that never happened. At about eight-thirty the phone rang. It was Adam Williams. He said he called an Andrew McGuire and a Carl McGuire before he found me. Then he apologized for calling so early.

I told him it didn't make any difference. I'd been up for hours. Then I blurted out what had happened with my toe, my father, and after, just for a moment, I wished I hadn't said anything. But then, it felt good to tell him about this morning. And that's when I agreed to have breakfast with Adam. Even my toe felt better, so I showered and dressed in jeans, a sweatshirt and flip-flops because the thought of putting on real shoes made my head hurt.

The doorbell bing-bongs, and I limp over, open it. Adam smiles at me, then his expression shows true concern.

"Hey, how's it going? Your dad come home yet?"

"No." I limp out the door.

We walk down the sidewalk to a red truck parked at the curb.

"Does your foot feel better?"

"A little." Actually it does. The ice must have helped.

"I used to stub my toe all the time when I was a kid. I'd race around barefoot and smack it. Hurt like hell, too." He starts to open my door to his truck, but I beat him to it. I don't want this to be a date.

After he settles on the driver's side, he looks over at me. "I brought some doughnuts, coffee. Thought we might go to the park. It's one of those great California days."

"You didn't have to buy all that stuff." I study him for a moment. He's smiling and, for a split second looks like the kid I remember in school.

"I didn't *buy* it. I said I *brought* it. I had company at my apartment till yesterday. It was left over."

"Oh." Guess he doesn't think this is a date, either.

"So's the park okay?"

"Sure."

We drive the short distance, talk about people we knew in school. Then Adam and I climb out of his truck and he retrieves a cardboard box from the back. "I didn't bring a blanket."

"Doesn't matter. We can sit on one of the benches." I wave toward the one near the lighthouse. We cut across the grass, me limping a little. Adam pulls out foam cups, a thermos of coffee, napkins, and takes the top off the doughnut box and puts it on the bench between us.

The doughnuts are stale but the coffee is excellent and I smile at him. He seems like a nice guy.

"You like it here?" he asks, gesturing toward the cliffs.

"It's okay. Thanks for breakfast," I say, holding up the coffee. "My mom loved this park—the lighthouse, especially. She said it brought people home, to their loved ones. I came here the other day, but it made me think about her too much."

"We can leave if you want."

I'm surprised I don't feel the way I did the other day—about to cry, lonesome. "No, I think I'm okay. This is good for me."

"She sounds like a nice lady."

"Yeah, she was."

"After we finish our coffee, I can take you to look for your father if you want."

I shake my head. "He's not a kid. What would I say? 'Get in the car. You're on restriction?'"

Adam laughs. "Now, that's an idea. But there's nothing wrong with checking on him, seeing if he's doing okay."

"We don't have that kind of relationship." I think about what kind of relationship we do have. It's always been uncomfortable, distant.

"He might like it that you're worried about him."

"I don't think so. We've never been close." I shake my head, wish getting along with my father were as easy as Adam makes it sound.

"Can you believe tomorrow's Christmas Eve?" he says.

I slap my forehead. "Oh, hell, I need to go shopping."

He blows on his coffee and wisps of steam curl up around his face. He looks at the lighthouse. "I can take you shopping."

"Don't you have to work?"

"I keep my own hours." This news does not surprise me.

"Thanks, I can go later." I think about the crowds, feel exhausted because I don't have any idea what to get my father. My mother used to do all my Christmas shopping so I wouldn't have to mail gifts or pack them if I was coming home.

"He'll like anything."

"What?"

"Your dad will like anything you get him and he'll be okay."

"How did you know I was thinking that?"

"You had this worried look on your face."

"When my mother was alive...I didn't have to worry about him or what to buy. She always knew what he needed."

Adam laughs. "He'll like whatever you get him. Heck, you're his daughter. Guys are like that. And he'll be okay because eventually we're all going to be okay. Things change, that's all. We have to accept change or we suffer. That's a tenet of Buddhism."

"Really?"

"Yeah, well something like that. But when we try to keep things the same, well, it's not good."

"*Change*. I came back here thinking things were going to be different, hoping my father and I would get along, maybe feel closer, since it's just he and I now, but nothing is different."

For a few moments, we drink our coffee, and I listen to the ocean rushing back and forth.

Suddenly, Adam gets off the bench, moves to the grass, lies down and looks up at the sky. "Look at those clouds! They're magnificent. Like an expensive painting, and it's all ours." He brings his arms up as if he's hugging something.

I glance up. "Looks like the same old sky to me."

Adam hops up and crosses the space between us. "Just look at the clouds. They're like puffs of dancing smoke…beautiful. They're alive! Something we'll never see again. Really look."

I give him a skeptical sidelong glance. "Is this part of the Buddhism you kind of know?"

He takes my hand, pulls me up. "It's your sky. Your world, grab it."

I look up again, I guess to thank him for the stale doughnuts and good coffee. The sky *is* beautiful with wonderful cloud formations, and to my surprise, excitement slides through me. I glance over at Adam and he raises his right eyebrow.

"See what I mean. It's all in the way you look at things."

It's after ten. I'm in my room taking off my sweatshirt. I put Adam's business card on the dresser. He handed it to me when he brought me home, told me if I needed anything at all to call him. Maybe I'm on his list of doing something nice for people. I probably won't call. There's Christmas, then the few days before New Year's Eve, then I'm gone.

Dad's still not home. I pull on a long-sleeved blue T-shirt. When I came in from the park, I called my office, checked my messages. Not one message. For some, no news is good news, but not for me. I guess things are quiet because of Christmas, which since I'm here, is a good thing.

I walk through the house, head out the front door. The cool air feels good. As cars go by, I check each one to see if it might be my father, but none of them are.

When I get to the park, it's still practically empty. A few joggers and a couple of stroller moms, but that's all. I sit on the bench by the lighthouse, grip the cold metal armrest. The ocean supplies background music for the drama going on inside my head. What the hell is my father planning? It would be so nice to talk to my mother about him. I rub my eyes, stand and walk halfway around the lighthouse before I see my father.

He's standing near the cliff, looking at papers he's holding. Before I can call out, the sun darts out from under a cloud and turns him silver—like an eye-catching ornament dangling from a Christmas tree.

"Hey."

He startles, looks at me for a long moment before he speaks. "Hey, honey."

"Did you go to the bank and City Hall?"

"Yeah, everything is set." He waves the paper at me.

"Set for what? You never told me." I hold my breath, hope it's something that will make us both happy and calm him down.

"I'm going to save the lighthouse."

I look at him, wait for a laugh. He doesn't. "Save this *lighthouse?*" I point to the wreck in front of us. "How are you going to do that?"

"My retirement money."

"*All* your money?" Obviously, he hasn't watched Suze Orman on TV.

"I'm doing it for your mother. She loved this place. The city was planning to tear it down. I couldn't let them do that. Your mother used to talk about how it brought people back home. You remember, don't you? How she loved the place?"

"Yeah, I remember." I move closer, take the paper, read some of it, then hand it back to him. It's a contract.

"I could have helped you negotiate this contract. You know that's what I do." I shake my head, feel hurt that he didn't ask me, didn't even think about it.

"I didn't want to bother you."

"That's obvious. I'm known as a really good negotiator in Tucson." My hurt mixes with anger, moves up to my throat and forms a knot.

"I did okay. But thanks for offering."

"You're going to use all your money? What about in a couple of years when you may need it?"

"I'll worry about a couple of years in a couple of years. I decided last night. Your mother loved the place, and I'm doing it for her. She deserves it."

CHAPTER 6

"Going out for your walk?" I ask my father, but don't know why. I know he is.

It's six o'clock. We finished dinner a little while ago. I went to the store this afternoon and bought a Stouffer's lasagna, a bag of salad, a bottle of blue cheese dressing and a *big* bottle of Chianti. I had a glass while I was setting the table, and then one with dinner, so I'm feeling pretty relaxed.

Dad is standing at the front door, looking like a man who wants to escape. He must have changed into his sweats and tennis shoes while I was doing the dishes.

"Yeah, thought I'd take a spin around the block." A somber tone edges every word.

All my life, he's been so serious. The Christmas tree lights blink on, then off.

"Dad, can we talk?"

"Let's do that later. I'll be back early, before you go to bed."

"I'm not sure this lighthouse deal is such a good idea," I blurt out. "Do you know how much money it's going to cost? I've seen my clients do renovations, and some of them have turned into complete messes. Both the project and the people."

He walks back across the room to where I'm sitting.

"Your mother deserves this, and that's what I want to do. There's room in there for me to live if I have to sell the house to get the renovation complete."

"But do you realize how much money and time the renovations are going to take? And if you have to sell the house, will you like living in a lighthouse?" I feel uneasy, intruding on my father's life. I've never given my father advice, and it feels weird doing it.

At dinner, he finally explained the deal the city made. He has to bring the lighthouse up to code in four weeks or they'll still tear it down and he'll be out the money. I think he paid too much for the place, but I didn't tell him that.

"The renovations aren't going to cost that much because I can do most of them myself. And what difference does it make where I live?"

"It makes a difference if you don't like it. Mom told me you guys were going to live on a lump sum from the airline. Is that what you're using to fund the project?"

He squints a little, as if he's surprised my mother shared this with me. "Yeah."

"The lighthouse is a wreck. Do you think you can bring it up to code in four weeks?"

"I'm going to try. This house is paid for." He glances around, then stares at a spot over my shoulder. "I can always sell it."

"But you have to pay taxes, there's still food, gas to buy, and the electric bill."

"I get social security in a couple of years."

"Not for three years! And it's not designed for you to live on."

"Two and a half."

I sigh, then laugh. "Whatever."

"Something funny?"

"This is funny. It used to be you telling me not to buy a new car, to save, to stay at a job. Now I'm advising you. There's something very ironic about all this. You've always been so sane, so dependable."

"I still am. I just can't let the city rip down the lighthouse. It wouldn't be right. Your mother wanted to get involved and I didn't listen to her. It's about time I do something irrational. Your mother would like that. Don't *you* care?"

"Of course I care, but this isn't like you and there's a limit to what we can do."

"I'm doing this." He crosses his arms.

"I know you don't believe this, but I know real estate. I've seen people get into—"

"With your brains you could have done anything."

Familiar anger begins to rise, but I manage to swallow it back. "Can we please get beyond what I didn't do and concentrate on what is going on now?"

"I wanted you to have what I didn't."

"I'm just saying it's not a good idea for you to take all your money and dump it into the lighthouse. You could lose everything."

"The lighthouse shouldn't be torn down." He

starts to sit down, then changes his mind and walks back to the front door.

I get up and go to where he is standing. "Dad, Mom had the sunniest, brightest outlook, but I don't think she'd want you to do this, put yourself in financial jeopardy and have all that work to do."

"I should have done what she wanted a long time ago, before it was too late." He shakes his head, steps back and looks out the window. "I don't care about the things I used to."

Before I can say anything else, he opens the front door and disappears.

Back on the couch, I look at the fake tree, the package I wrapped for him a little while ago. This afternoon, I went Christmas shopping—which, by then, I wasn't in the mood for—but I did find my father a blue pullover sweater. I figure he can wear it when he's walking.

I cross my arms. The house is almost noiseless. The yellow quilted pillow my mother made years ago sits in the corner by the TV. All her things, everything she loved, are still here. Why in the world did I think coming home without my mother here would turn out okay? I thought I had gotten over the intense grief, wouldn't argue with my father like before, and maybe, just maybe, we could build some sort of relationship.

I get up, walk down the hall toward my room. At my mother's small bathroom across from their bedroom, I turn on the light, go in. There is no Jacuzzi tub, no marble countertop. The room is 1930s Depression plain—white sink, square-mirrored medicine cabinet, oversize white tub, and it reminds me so much of my mother. If something were to happen to my father, what would remind me of him? I shake my head. I'm not sure.

A tray of colored jars and bottles, like a rainbow in a plain sky, is the only bright spot. I sit at the vanity, lift the chubby Obsession bottle, take off the cap and sniff. The scent is rich and hopeful. I look in the mirror and half expect her to be standing behind me.

Crazy.

I place the bottle back on the clean circle surrounded by dust, pick up a jar and run my finger over the raised letters *La Crème De Visage Croient*. Then I remove the translucent aquamarine lid. The cream inside is the color of a cucumber.

I slide the lever on my mother's makeup mirror to *Evening Lite*, click it on, reach back and turn off the overhead light. A muted pink paints the walls, the sink, me. I dab some cucumber-colored cream on my chin, rub it in while I'm looking in the mirror.

A memory surfaces—I'm standing in this room, next to her, asking little girl questions—*Why do you always use the pink light?* She touches my cheek, tells me it makes her prettier. I asked if it makes me prettier, too, and she laughs, explains I'm always beautiful, pink inside and out. Then I ask how pretty my father is.

She looks at me for a long moment, tilts her head against mine—*Never forget he needs you to love him. When he was little he wasn't loved very much.*

My head begins to throb. I flip off the stupid Evening Lite, bring my hands to the sides of my face and watch shadows dance. How do I love my father as much as my mother wanted me to when I don't believe he loves me very much at all?

"You've been out so long. Don't you think you should come home?" I ask Dad.

The ocean breeze brushes tendrils of hair against my face. After waiting two hours for him and drinking another glass of wine, I walked down to the park. Now we're standing in front of the lighthouse.

I point the flashlight I'm holding at him. He squints, presses his lips together, and I feel bad for making him uncomfortable, so I shift the light to the ground.

"You shouldn't have walked here by yourself," he says. "It's late."

"I wouldn't have had to if you would come home." My mother's words thump through my mind, *love him*. I clench my jaw, unclench it and try to smile, but I can't.

"Don't worry about me. I took a long walk then I thought I'd come here, look around. That's all. I've got a lot to do."

I brush my hair out of my face. "I still think we need to talk about this." I gesture to the lighthouse, look at it, then focus on my father. "If you come home I'll make you some hot chocolate."

"This place," he says, pointing to the beacon as if he doesn't really hear me. "I can't wait to get started, get the light to come on."

"Well, you can't start tonight." My entire body feels fatigued and I sit on the bench, one hand on my thigh, the other still holding the flashlight. It would be so easy to go back to the house, take a hot bath, sleep till noon and let him do what he wants. Then, after Christmas, I could go home, sell more houses, make people happy who want me to help them.

"You okay?" he asks, then takes the flashlight from me, and the fingerlike beam melts into the darkness.

A gust of wind pushes him forward a little.

More fatigue saturates my body. "I miss Mom so much." It slips out, outlined in grief. I close my eyes, push back my sad feelings, then stand and cross my arms.

"I'm going home and going to bed. It's too windy out here. I'll see you tomorrow."

I don't wait for him to say anything. I walk around the bench, across the grass, feel so lonely, really hollow inside. I stop and rub my eyes.

"What's wrong?" He's walked across the grass to me.

I look at him. "Nothing. I just want to go home." I jam my hands into my pockets.

"You shouldn't be walking alone at night."

"I'm fine." I begin walking again and my dad joins me. We walk back home in silence.

"Hi, it's Sandra."

My father and I got back from the park ten minutes ago. I let the phone ring, thinking Dad would answer it, but he didn't, so I picked it up on the sixth ring.

"Hi, how are you?"

"Okay. I was wondering what you're doing? Hope I didn't call too late. I saw your lights on."

"No, I was up."

"I'm going to see Mama. Want to come with me?"

"This late?" I ask.

"Yeah, I go up there all the time at night. It's not far, just right up by the drugstore."

I think about being with someone who's fun, riding in a car, not worrying about my father, and how much visiting has changed since my mother passed away.

"Yeah, I'll go."

"We won't be gone long. Put on a sweatshirt and

I'll meet you out front in five minutes. With the holidays, it might be the only time you have to see her."

In the living room, Dad is sitting in his chair, watching TV.

"That was Sandra. I'm going with her to visit Josephine."

"Good, honey, go ahead, glad you girls are getting together," he says, without looking at me.

I head to my bedroom and find an old sweatshirt I left here years ago and drape it over my shoulders.

"We'll only be gone for a little while," I say after I walk back to the living room. I go to the front door, stop, turn back. "Would you like to come with us?" I don't want him along, but I feel that I should ask.

"No. You girls spend some time together." The Christmas tree lights snap on then off, and I walk out onto the porch.

Josephine's familiar white Cadillac is sitting in the dark drive. I cross the grass, feel the slippery dew through the soles of my tennis shoes. When I reach the car I look in the open window and laugh.

"Why do you have the headlights off? It's like we're making a drug deal."

"I wish. I didn't want to disturb your dad."

"He's watching TV. Nothing would disturb him," I say as I climb in the car. "Isn't it funny, no matter how old I am, when I'm around my parents, I feel like a kid." I stop, realize I've said *parents*. "I mean when I'm around Dad, you know when my mother was…" I feel awkward. I've known Sandra for a long time, but my living in Tucson has put so much space between us.

"I know what you mean." She backs out of the drive, heads toward town, then turns the lights on. "I drive my mother's car once in a while to keep it going—one never knows." She smiles. "Should we cruise town?"

I laugh. "Remember how we used to borrow your mother's car, tell her we were going to the library and then drive all over San Pedro?"

"How could I forget? Remember we bought gas so my dad wouldn't know?"

"Yeah, we were so cagey."

"He knew. He told me about twenty years ago that he caught on to what we were doing. Like we were so smart."

"Oh, God."

"Don't worry. He didn't care. Neither did she. They were cool parents."

Sandra drives slowly through the streets that were imprinted on my mind years ago. San Pedro is on a peninsula, and it feels as if it's at the edge of the earth. It is a town filled with houses built in the early 1920s and thirties, quaint, comfortable, nothing flashy, but each unique.

Four blocks from our house, I realize I'm happy to be away. And for a quick moment, I feel like I did when I was thirteen and Sandra was sixteen, free, excited about growing up with so many things to look forward to. I look over at her. We shared so many things, but we probably don't have that much in common anymore.

"I never realized how dark the streets are," I say, continuing to look out the window and watch the eclectic blend of architecture move past. "The nursing home won't care if you visit so late?"

"I know the swing nurses and the security guard. I go up there most nights, you know, just to check on her." She flicks her hand in the dashboard light. "What else do I have to do?"

Sandra's voice is strong, but at the edge of her words I hear pain—something I'm familiar with.

"I'm sorry about your mother," I say. "It must be so hard on you."

"At least I still have her here." Even in the dim light, I see her eyes narrow, know what she means.

"Yeah," I say softly. I turn on the radio, glance at Sandra. "You care?"

"Of course not."

"Blue Christmas" flows through the speakers, Elvis's voice, smooth, mesmerizing. "Christmas music. Does it get to you?"

"Yes!" She looks over at me, nods and laughs. Sandra points to the radio. "But I like this one. 'I'll have a *bluuuueee* Christmas without you. I'll be *soooo* blue thinking about you....'"

We sing softly with Elvis, drive north on Western Avenue, away from the ocean, toward the hospital. The night air reminds me how my mother and Josephine would sit in the kitchen in the evenings, turn on the radio and talk, their soft voices braiding with the music. The sounds traveled through the house to Sandra's bedroom. Those evenings were comforting, knowing our mothers were in the next room. I never thought about it ending.

In the care-center parking lot, three cars sit by the street, spotlighted in the glassy light.

"You always come up here alone at night?" I ask.

"Yeah. When I'm home, I wonder how she is, if she's okay, and I get in the car and then I'm here."

She parks, turns off the engine. The quiet saturates us. For a moment, we just sit, me with my hands in my lap, Sandra clutching the steering wheel.

"You know, I never thought my life would be like this." Sandra turns a little, looks toward the facility. "Remember how my mother was always joking, telling funny stories?"

I nod. Sandra doesn't move.

"Now she can't remember who I am. I used to come here during the day and take her out for coffee, to the Starbucks on Pacific, but each time she'd get more afraid, more apprehensive. Then I realized I was just taking her out to make myself feel better, so I stopped."

I breathe, unclasp my hands, don't know what to say.

Sandra turns to me. "I'm fine. And I certainly don't mean to lay this all on you."

"That's okay." But I'm glad when we get out of the car.

The cool air feels good against my hot face, hands. I can see our breaths, white cone shapes drifting from our lips. At the door, Sandra rings the bell. A man, in his early thirties, comes to the front. When he sees Sandra, he smiles, opens the door.

"How ya doing, Bernard?" Sandra asks.

"Fine. Your mama is okay tonight, not as bad as last week. Loellen is on duty." He motions toward the back of the facility. "Good to see you."

We walk down the shiny hall, turn left, stop in front of a nurses' station. There is a small fake Christmas tree in the far corner with childlike paper decorations. I wonder if the decorations are from Point Fermin Elementary where Sandra and I went to school.

A young African American woman dressed in a white lab coat and pants looks up, smiles.

"Hey." Her voice is like glass, hard yet smooth and beautiful.

"Hey, yourself." Sandra leans across the counter, takes the woman's hand and holds it for a minute. A strong connection. She introduces us and I smile.

"How's my mother?" Sandra asks.

"She's okay. I just checked on her. She's sitting in her chair. I gave her the new night meds the doctor ordered last week and she calmed down. Go on in."

I follow Sandra around the corner and we stop not far from the nurses' station. The door to room 316 is open, and we walk in.

Josephine is sitting in a red chair, one I remember from her living room. The light is on and she is staring out the window. I see her reflection on the glass, her familiar expression, large eyes and full lips, and I think about my mother.

She looks startled for a moment, then touches Sandra's mirror image with the tips of her fingers.

"Mama," Sandra says, sounding like the young girl I remember. She crosses the room and gives her mother a hug.

Her mother smiles like a child, nods. "Do I know you?"

"Yes, Mama. I'm Sandra, your daughter. Remember?"

The last word touches my heart. Then Josephine looks at me.

"Hello." Yet her eyes question her daughter.

"Hi," I say, trying to sound upbeat. I swallow over the lump in my throat.

"Mama, this is Christine, from next door. Remember her?"

Josephine nods, but looks at her hands.

"Hi, Mrs. Jackson." I don't know what else to do, so I sit on the edge of the hospital bed with a smile pasted on my face.

Josephine looks at Sandra again. "Are we related or what?"

"You're my mama and I'm your daughter."

"Okay."

"You need your hair combed," Sandra says. She goes to the small bathroom on the other side of the room and comes back with a brush. She sits on the arm of the large chair, begins brushing her mother's hair.

"What did you do today?" Sandra asks.

"I don't know."

I watch them and suddenly I realize Sandra and I have more in common than I thought—we have both lost our mothers.

CHAPTER 7

It's Christmas Eve morning and I'm listening to Diane Sawyer talk about special Christmas breakfasts for families. Her advice: families should get together and enjoy one another over breakfast Christmas morning. I plugged in the tree when I first got up, and about three minutes ago it started blinking like crazy, totally out of control.

I hear the back door open. I get up and go to the kitchen. Dad has poured coffee into his mug. He takes a big sip. At least his hair is combed and he's dressed in clean clothes.

He looks up, sees me and smiles. "What do you want to do tonight?"

"Have dinner, I guess." My mother always made a big turkey dinner on Christmas Eve, even if it was just she and I. Then we'd eat leftovers Christmas Day, wait for Dad to come home if he was on a trip.

I loved Christmases with my mother. They were warm, fun, something to look forward to.

"We could bake a ham," Dad says, rubbing the side of his face.

"I guess we could."

"You know how to cook one?"

"Not really. I eat out a lot. But I could look in Mom's cookbook." My mother was a good cook, and she seemed to enjoy it. It's obvious I didn't inherit that trait from her.

"I eat out a lot, too."

I nod, look toward the living room and the tree, watch the tree lights blink their crazy pattern. "Did you see the tree?" I nod toward the living room and Dad looks. "It started a little while ago."

"I'll see if I can fix them later. It would probably be easier to go out. What do you think?" He pours his coffee into the sink, rinses the cup, then heads to the back door.

"Probably. I don't mind going out."

"Good, then that's what we'll do. I've got some errands. I'll be home later."

And before I can say anything about how, since

it's Christmas Eve day, maybe we could spend some time together, he's out the door.

I heard the Volvo pull in the driveway a little while ago, and I'm sitting on the couch waiting for Dad to come into the house. Most of the day, I sat and watched TV, slept a little and checked my phone messages five times. There were no messages about any of my list-ings. By three, everyone in the office had gone home. I love when the phone rings and I get to negotiate a sale. But during the holiday, people are busy.

Dad walks into the living room, looks at the dark tree, goes over and plugs in the lights. They pop on, mix with the glow from the table lamp, then begin blinking erratically, just as they did this morning before I unplugged the darned things.

"Merry Christmas," I say. An hour ago, I show-ered, put on black slacks, a red sweater that I bought two weeks ago for tonight. That's when I began feeling a little excited, kind of like when I was a kid. Sandra called this morning, and I asked if she wanted to come over and go out to dinner with us, but she told me she was spending the evening at the nursing home with her mother.

Dad sits in his chair, sighs, notices the Christmas tree lights. "What the hell is wrong with that tree?"

"I told you about it this morning, remember? It started right after I plugged it in. I unplugged it, then tried it again and gave up."

"I'll fix it later. I'm beat."

"Big day?" I ask.

"Yeah." He rubs his face.

"Did you find out anything more about the lighthouse?" I'm hoping someone at City Hall told him they've changed their minds and he needs to forget about this crazy deal, but deep down I know this isn't going to happen.

"City's all for it. Plus Chet says he's going to help me."

My heart sinks more. Dad gets up, goes over to the tree, pulls a branch that's at a strange angle, then bends it a little too hard. The Santas sway dangerously and blinking red light strobes through the room. He grabs the tree, steadies it before it falls off the table.

"That was a close one."

"Yeah." He kneels and pulls the plug from the wall. When he stands, he looks at me. "I guess we should open presents."

My attention moves to under the tree—the three gifts. All my life, my mother and I, and sometimes my father, when he was home, would open presents on Christmas morning. There were always lots of presents, all different shapes and sizes, wrapped in pretty Christmas paper. Mom always went overboard and I loved it.

"Well?" Dad asks.

"I guess we could have Christmas now," I say as my heart begins to beat a little faster.

"Your mother told me that when I wasn't here, you and she would open one present on Christmas Eve."

I take a deep breath and memories of past Christmases rush at me—Dad on a trip, my mother and I drinking hot chocolate, sitting on the floor by the tree, laughing. We would open one small package on Christmas Eve, save the rest for morning.

"So what do you want to do?" he asks, his question breaking into my reminiscing.

"I'm not sure. I guess we could have our Christmas now."

"Okay."

He gets up, goes to the tree, kneels and picks up the two small red-and-white packages. For a moment, he looks so old. My mother always seemed so young, her dark hair swaying with her laughter. There were times she was serious, when I'd ask a question or when she was talking about my father, but she never looked old.

Dad struggles up, sits on the opposite end of the couch. He hands me the larger, oblong package. "Might as well get this over with. Here you go."

"Now, that's the Christmas spirit." Dad doesn't laugh, or even smile. I take the box, shake it a little. No sound. "Isn't this the first present you've ever bought me?"

"What do you mean? I bought you lots of presents through the years." He gestures to where our big tree used to stand. "There were way too many presents every year."

"I know. I'm not complaining. But this is the first time *you* picked out something for me."

Dad looks at the package in my hand and then

at me. "You're right. Your mother used to buy me things from you, too."

"You knew?"

"Yeah."

"And we thought we were fooling you. Mom just wanted to make it easy for me when I came for Christmas, or when I couldn't come home."

Dad finally smiles. "She liked doing that."

I slowly unwrap the package. Then I open the box and find a ladies' Cross pen and pencil set, black, nice, a sensible gift.

"Thanks, Dad." I scoot over, give him an awkward hug, move back. I take the pen out of its holder, twist it open then closed.

"You can use them?"

"Of course. I love it. I always need a pen. I'll keep this one in my purse and the pencil, too. They'll be lucky for me." I put the pen back in the box.

"People make their own luck."

"I know, but I believe in luck, too. In the real estate business, you have to believe in luck. Open mine now." I get up and take the package I wrapped over to him.

He pulls the paper off, unfolds the soft blue sweater, holds it up to his shoulders. "I need this."

"I thought you could wear it when you walk."

Then there is silence. And I feel like we are inexperienced actors forgetting our lines.

"There's one more," he finally says, and slides the smaller box across the couch.

This is it, then Christmas will be over. The first Christmas without my mother—hollow, flat. But what did I expect?

I undo the crisp paper. The small square box is dark brown, the size of my hand. In an effort to create more of a Christmas mood, I bring it to my ear, shake it. I hear a *thunk, thunk, thunk*.

"Interesting."

Dad half smiles and my heart aches. I lift the lid. No tissue or cotton. The box contains my mother's silver key chain that has always had a tiny flashlight attached to the ring. The light rolls from one side to the other, and a small lump forms in my throat. I'd forgotten about this—she used it for as long as I can remember.

I pick up the small flashlight, click it on, then off, run my index finger over the familiar engraving: *Stay safe Love Jake*. When I was little, I would run my thumbnail in the etched lines.

You're going to wear the letters off, Chrissy.

"It was your mother's," Dad says, and his words shift me from her world to his.

"It runs on a triple A battery. I put a fresh one in the other day before I wrapped it."

"I'd forgotten about it."

"After the police officer gave it to me, I put it in her top drawer. I was going through some things three weeks ago…" He crosses his arms, looks down at the key chain. "I bought it for her after you were born. I couldn't be home at night…she needed a light to help her…I worried about her."

I open my hand and look at the inscription again.

"I used to play with it all the time. When I learned how to read, I asked Mom if it was a reminder to love you. You know like a command, *love Jake*. She laughed, explained what it meant."

"I told her I'd have the commas put in, but she said she liked it that way. When I ticked her off, she'd read it and laugh."

I hold the key chain up by the silver ring, and it moves back and forth. "Her car keys were on this?"

Dad nods and I think about my mother on the freeway, all alone, the silver glinting, swaying. We look at each other, and I know by his expression, he's thinking the same thing.

He stands, jams his hands in his pockets. "I'm going to take a quick walk."

"But I thought we were going out to dinner?"

"It's early. I need some fresh air."

There's deep pain in his voice. He walks across the living room toward the kitchen, and I feel a little light-headed, don't know what to do, so I follow him, touch his arm when we reach the kitchen.

"Don't leave," I say. "It's Christmas Eve."

"I'll be back soon, just need some fresh air."

"You always left," I say, then wish I hadn't. Why can't I just keep my big mouth shut? But my hurt is overriding any control I have. I want him to want to stay here and enjoy the evening. Maybe even ask me about my work, my life, how much I miss Mom.

"What?"

"This is just like when Mom was alive, except now she isn't here. You were always gone."

"I had to work."

"All the time? That's pretty much bull," I say, wishing I were back in Tucson and not feeling so fully exposed, unbuttoned. I close my fingers and my mother's key chain channels into my skin.

Dad goes to the back door, then turns toward me. "I got better flights. Your mother said it was okay, that you and she did okay. I never liked Christmas."

"But she loved it. Did you ever think that she was just saying that?"

"Everybody makes mistakes. Like not calling when you could have." He shakes his head, as though he's sorry he said the last part. But I feel like cold water has been thrown on me.

"You didn't need to bring that up. It's Christmas."

"We'll go out to dinner in a little while. I just want to check on the lighthouse."

"What needs checking on? It's an empty building. I'm here. I came home to keep you company."

Dad takes a step toward me, then stops. "I guess I just need to be alone for a while."

"Do you realize how much I miss her?"

He stares at me, like he's not sure what to say next, what to do. And in a blink of an eye, he's gone.

* * *

It's 9:00 a.m. Christmas Day. I slept late, but still feel exhausted. I don't know where my father is. His bedroom door is closed, and I don't have the energy to check on him. We went to dinner last night, when he finally came home at eight. By the time we got to Ventanos, the place was closed.

All we could find open was a Pizza Hut, and I ended up having two large glasses of cheap wine and almost said, *"Merry f'ing Christmas,"* but I didn't, thank goodness. I kept my mouth shut, so we didn't argue anymore or even talk about our conversation in the kitchen.

Between last night and this morning, I've checked my cell phone and office messages ten times. No messages on either. I even used Dad's phone and called my cell and the office to see if they were both working.

The doorbell rings, I startle, knock the side of my yellow mug, and an amoeba-like splotch spreads on the napkin underneath.

"Damn," I say, then find another napkin and mop up the mess.

At the front door, Adam Williams smiles at me, holds up a brown paper bag with one of those sticky red bows pasted at the top.

"Merry Christmas," he says.

"Adam?"

"Yeah. It's me." He smiles again. "Is it too early?"

"No, I'm just surprised to see you." I step out onto the porch, leave the door open. Early morning sunshine drenches me, and I squint until I visor my eyes.

"Wow, it's bright out here."

"Yeah. It's a great day. I bought this for you yesterday," he says, and lifts the bag again. "I was going to come by, but I was working on a project."

"You didn't have to do that."

"I know, but I wanted to." He bounces the bag a little.

I realize I should invite him in. After last night with my father, the wine, I feel empty, tired, so played out, I guess I'm not thinking very fast.

"Why don't you come in?" I walk into the house.

Adam stands in the living room, his arms down by his sides.

"Please, sit down."

"Here." He hands me the bag. I unfold it and pull out a bag of Starbucks coffee. "Hope you like their Christmas Blend."

"Thanks. I do. This is so thoughtful. Would you like some?"

"Nah, I just came by to see how you're doing. Check on your toe. Did you have a good Christmas?"

I laugh, wiggle my foot. "It's fine, and yes, I did." I think about telling him about last night, but then I remember we barely know each other.

"How was your Christmas Eve?" I ask instead.

"It was okay."

"Were you with your family?"

"My mother passed away three years ago. Never knew my father. My holidays are pretty quiet. I went to see an uncle in Hermosa Beach, and we ordered a pizza and drank a couple of beers."

He looks around the room, then back to me. "You sure everything is okay? I wasn't planning on stopping by, but this morning I thought about you, wondered if you were doing all right. And I wanted to give you the coffee."

The concern on his face touches my heart, opens it up a little, and I relax a bit more.

"My father's decided to renovate the old lighthouse to honor my mother. That's what he was checking on the other day when I hurt my foot."

"Good for him."

I rub my face and wonder if I'm worrying for nothing. I glance up, and Adam smiles at me.

"Not my reaction. It's just that he's taking all his savings to do it, plus it has to be up to code in four weeks. I've seen people take on these kinds of projects renovating houses, and a lot of times they don't work out."

"Have you talked to him about your concerns?"

"Till I'm blue in the face, but he went to the city and they're all for it. He signed a contract without letting me look at it! He used to be so practical."

"Maybe it'll work."

"Something is just not right with him. He's never been sentimental. He says he's doing it for my mother. I understand that, but it's irrational. He was a pilot, not a person who knows a lot about construction."

"Three years ago, my sixty-eight-year-old uncle

MARY SCHRAMSKI   129

left his wife of thirty-five years for a lap dancer from Van Nuys. Fixing up a lighthouse is mild compared to that."

"Same uncle you saw last night?"

"No." Adam laughs. "I was with the sane one."

"The lighthouse is a wreck. I keep wondering if it's my responsibility to talk him out of it, if I should be meddling?"

"How long has your mother been gone?"

"Eight months." I expect Adam to talk about Buddhism, Zen, something off the wall.

"Some people never recover from losing someone they love."

I nod. "I know."

"And the money—it owns you, you don't own it. Maybe your dad realizes that. When we grasp, we cause ourselves misery."

"A tenet of Buddhism?" I ask, then smile.

He laughs again. "No, that's an *Adamism*."

I hear the back door open, then shut. A moment later, my father is standing in the living room. I introduce him to Adam.

Adam gets up, extends his hand. "Sir, it's nice to meet you."

"*Sir?* Name's Jake," he says, sniffs. "It smells like coffee in here."

"Adam brought us Starbucks, for Christmas." I hold up the bag, swing it a little. "Where'd you go?"

"I'm working on a list of supplies I need. I'm going to need a lot of wiring." He looks at me, then Adam.

"Wiring for electrical work?" Adam asks.

"Yeah, a lot."

"I'm an electrical engineer."

Dad studies him for a moment. "I might want to talk to you about a job. Did Christine tell you about the lighthouse?"

"Yeah."

"Think you could help me with the electrical work?"

Adam shrugs, looks at me, then back to my father. "I'd have to check it out first."

"Great. I'd better get going. I've got a lot to do."

"Where are you…?" But before I can finish my question he's gone.

I look at Adam, raise an eyebrow. "And that's been my life for the past few days."

CHAPTER 8

I'm sitting in the kitchen, thinking how thankful I am that Dad and I made it through Christmas Day without any more arguments. This morning, I woke up at five, checked my mes-sages, stared at my cell phone for a moment, surprised it hasn't rung once since I've been here. Then I showered and dressed. I heard Dad in the shower when I was walking down the hall.

The swinging door opens and he walks into the kitchen.

"Good morning," I say, singsong, trying to be up-beat, determined not to argue anymore. He's combed his hair, but it needs trimming and it makes him look like a kid. A tiny ache, not as big as a button, pulses in my chest.

"Morning," he says.

He leans against the counter, takes a deep breath

as if he's working to build up enough energy to stay and talk to me. He has a lot of get-up-and-go when it comes to the lighthouse, but I guess not enough for me.

"Tired?" I ask.

"Yeah. How long have you known Adam?"

"What?"

"Adam. How long have you known him?"

I sit straighter, look at him. Is he worried that I'm dating someone? My mother was always the one to give me advice on dating, my love life. I hope he's not starting now!

"I went to high school with him. But I don't really *know* him."

"Did he come around then?" Dad straightens, crosses his arms.

"No. Why are you asking?"

"Why did he come over yesterday?" he asks, ignoring my question.

"Because when you left the other day, I stubbed my toe and I told him about it and he was worried. He's a nice guy."

"Is he reliable?"

"I don't know. Probably. I'm not interested in

him, if that's what you're worried about. And if you've forgotten, I am over forty."

"I know how old you are. I was thinking about hiring him to do the electrical work on the lighthouse."

"Oh."

"If he can do the wiring—"

"About the lighthouse, would you explain to me what your plan is? I mean…have you really thought this through?"

"I'm going to bring the lighthouse back to the way it was, the way your mother wanted it. I don't care about the money or the work. Your mother is the focus." He starts toward the back door.

"Dad, I'm not sure Mom—"

He turns around, looks at me. "I'm doing this for her. You, most of all, should understand that. I spent my life pushing her to be practical. I think she might get a kick out of this."

"She wouldn't want you to spend all your money."

"Don't you think your mother deserves this?"

"Of course I do but—"

"But what?" His eyes narrow, as if he's trying to understand what I'm thinking.

"I'm just worried, that's all."

"Nothing to worry about. I've got the money and the time."

"Where are you going now?" I'm lonely, and for the first time, I realize I've always ached for my father's attention that he doesn't seem to want to give me.

"I'm going to the park."

"Are you walking?"

"Yeah."

"Mind if I go along? I don't have anything to do."

"No, if you want to."

We walk down Thirty-eighth Street in bright winter sunshine. Thank God I brought my sunglasses. Dad is really hauling it, and I'm struggling to keep up. He's actually in better shape than I am. By the time we get to Forty-second, I'm out of breath and I stumble off the curb, but catch myself before I fall.

Dad takes my elbow to steady me. "You okay?"

"I'd be better if you weren't almost running. Where's the fire? You're walking as if you're on a mission."

He laughs softly. "Sorry, you should have said something."

We walk across the grassy area, then stop at the bench in front of the lighthouse. Dad pulls keys out of his pocket.

"Are those the lighthouse keys?"

"Yeah. I picked them up this morning. Now I can really get started." He studies the keys for a moment, then looks back to me. "Christine, it's going to be okay."

"This is just such a big commitment, a lot of work and not very much time."

"But saving her—" he gestures toward the tower "—is something I really want to do. You don't have to stay. I'm just going to look around for a while, then I'll be home."

I would like to go back to the house, not worry about him, but something in me won't let me leave. I shake my head. "I'll stay. I've never seen the inside. Mom told me about it, though."

We walk to the front of the lighthouse. The gate squeaks as Dad pushes it open. "I need to fix that." He nods toward it.

"And probably about a million other things."

"Yeah, but my first priority is the beacon. I want that working as soon as possible. Your mother dreamed of the light coming on. Then I'm going to spruce up the inside." Dad keys the padlock, pushes on the door. It opens without the groan I expect.

Slashes of sunlight from the glass dome cut through the darkness, dance against the top of the battered walls. In the dim light, I can see two doors across from the entry. They probably lead to the living quarters. In the middle of the room is a metal staircase leading to the top.

"I should have brought a flashlight," Dad says, squinting.

"I have Mom's." I dig it out of my pocket, click it on. It's small and doesn't add much light to the room, but when I look at Dad's expression, I know he's stunned by the damage. The walls are crumbling and there's trash all over.

"Maybe it's good you don't have a flashlight. There's a lot of *sprucing* to do."

"It is pretty bad."

"So can you get your money back?"

"I don't want my money back. The place will be

great when I bring her back to life." Dad finds a loose brick and props open the door. More light from the outside tumbles in and highlights the damage.

"I can see why the Coast Guard and the city wanted to tear it down," I say.

"Their loss." He moves to the middle of the room, puts his hand on the staircase. "Look at these stairs."

"They look dangerous."

"A little sanding and paint, they'll be like new." Dad puts his foot on the first step, and we both hear a huge creak and the scraping of metal.

I grab his arm. His body is so warm. "I don't think that's such a good idea."

His attention remains on the sunlit circle above. "Yeah, maybe not."

"I'm glad you realize that."

"I'll get to the stairs as soon as I can."

"Dad?"

"Yeah?"

Finally, he looks at me. "Maybe you could take a break today, and we could do something together. Drive to L.A., have lunch. Mom and I used to do that when I'd visit."

"I've got a lot of work." His attention shifts again to the glass dome. "It's good none of those panes are broken. I thought they might be."

I have five more days before I leave, to go back to Tucson, to my life. That's not a lot of time to get to know my father, build some sort of relationship, especially if he doesn't want to do anything with me. And suddenly, as if a light has been turned on inside me, I feel foolish for bothering him, for trying to get close, for even being here.

"You know, I think I'll go on back to the house," I say, and walk out the door.

Jake sat on the bench. Sunset slashed the pale sky, and shadows from the trees moved against the grass and one another. He was tired, yet the fatigue felt gratifying. Today he'd gone to Home Depot, ordered Sheetrock, bought a ladder and supplies, and had cleared out the debris. He must have hauled twenty trash bags to the dump.

He leaned back, groaned and rubbed his right hip. He'd fallen from the metal steps a few minutes ago, landed on his side, and now his hip hurt.

Standing, he rubbed his hip again and winced.

He closed his eyes, then looked out toward the park and growing shadows. All he wanted was to see Dorothy and feel happy.

Jake shook his head. For years, he'd trained himself to accept reality. That's how he stayed alive when he was flying fighters and commercial jets. In flight school his instructor had told him, *"Don't let your mind play games with your reality."*

And now…he looked at the lighthouse. This idea of bringing the place back to the way it once was wasn't practical. He rubbed his sore hip and felt old. What the hell was he doing spending money on the lighthouse, thinking he could fix the problems? Maybe Christine was right. And he couldn't ignore the way she'd looked at him. It was obvious she thought he was acting like an idiot. She was worried, and he certainly didn't want to worry her. He hadn't been a very good father, and he didn't want to be any kind of burden to her now.

He gazed at the unlit beacon, then limped over to the grassy area of the park. He needed to go home, think things through, maybe change his mind and get himself out of this deal.

"Hey."

He turned around, toward the sound, then smiled. Dorothy was standing in front of him, not eight feet away. He drank in her dark hair, the red dress she loved, her smile.

And then, too soon, she was gone.

But Jake felt warm, happy, the way he had when he'd come home and Dorothy was waiting for him on the tiny porch of their first apartment. He always parked in the same spot on the street, and she'd wave, say *hey* and smile her great smile. And, at that moment, he knew he was loved, for the first time in his life.

More feelings melted through him, saturated his body and pooled in his chest until he thought he was going to burst with happiness. It was so good to see her again.

Jake walked back to the park bench, closed his eyes and savored the image. Years ago, right after Christine had been born, Dorothy had slid that same red dress to the back of her closet because it was too small. She'd said one day she'd wear it again.

One day.

He'd never told her how much he admired her hope, her faith.

Jake looked up at the dark sky. Did she know how he felt now? Could she see him? He wasn't sure what he believed anymore.

His body tightened, the rhythm of his breath increased. The knot in his throat grew and he began crying. Dorothy was the only person he'd ever cared about. Why did she have to die? All he ever wanted was to live out his life with her by his side. Why couldn't he have been the one on the freeway? Was that asking too much?

She'd always told him to believe in fate, to know there was a pattern, *a time to live, a time to die*, she'd said when her mother had passed away.

She'd been so centered, trusting.

How could he have thought about not completing the lighthouse for her?

And after?

"A time to live, a time to die," he whispered.

"Maybe you need to realize that he isn't going to take your suggestions," Sandra says. "And we have no idea what he's thinking."

Sandra and I have walked to the Port Fermin Café for an early dinner. She called me this morning from work and asked me if I wanted to join her. I knew Dad wouldn't be home, so I figured why not. As I was getting ready, I remembered when we were kids our mothers would fix us dinner really early and call it "linner," a combination of lunch and dinner.

The restaurant is almost empty except for the young waitress who reminds me of high school, the cook and an older couple, sitting in a booth, arguing about money. Engelbert Humperdinck's voice parades through the room as he sings "After the Loving."

Sandra glances back to the couple as their voices rise, then she turns around.

"How old do you think that couple is?"

I shake my head. "I don't know, sixties, maybe."

"Aren't they a little old to be fighting in a restaurant?"

"I guess." I look around and I'm glad I'm here. This morning, after walking through the lighthouse, I walked back home, realized everyone I knew in San Pedro was at work, so I cleaned the house and checked for messages. There was only one—a referral client who wants to start looking for three-bedroom condos next month. I called her back, set a date for late January and then continued cleaning.

I usually clean when I'm frustrated, and the house needed it. I hung up Dad's clothes, vacuumed, did the bathrooms, three loads of wash, and ironed. Then I attacked the kitchen. I wiped off the cabinets, cleaned the refrigerator and mopped all the floors. But it was weird cleaning without Mom. It was almost as if I could hear her voice. By the time I finished, Sandra had come home from work.

"You should see the lighthouse, the stairs alone are a major health hazard. And we got in an argument this morning," I say.

"About what?" Sandra's forehead creases.

"Oh, it wasn't a screaming match. I don't know. Yes, I do. He insinuated I don't care about my mother's memory. Can you believe that?"

"Sounds like he's mixed up. This lighthouse gig—" Sandra takes a sip of her Coke, looks at me over the straw "—you know, he might feel guilty about your mother."

There it is.

The elephant in the room I've been trying to ignore, not talk about. But I've thought this, too.

"I guess that's a possibility."

"*Possibility?* Tine? I got to know your mother pretty well in the last couple of years. She helped me with Mama, talked to me, was really supportive. We became good friends." Sandra studies the table, then looks up.

"And?" I ask.

"This is when life gets difficult."

"What do you mean by *that?*"

"How do I tell you how unhappy your mother was with your father?"

"My mother was unhappy?"

"Yeah."

The times I saw my parents together, my mother was usually smiling, laughing; my father, calm, even. "What do you mean by *unhappy?*"

"She would just say things. She'd come over for coffee or we'd go to lunch after seeing Mama, and she'd say things."

"What do you mean by *things?*" I think back, remember our phone calls, how good she always sounded. How she'd always say my father was fine, life was great.

"Now you've got me scared. Did he abuse her?"

"No, of course not."

I nod, try to digest this information. It's odd to think of her as my mother's friend, too.

"Tine, your mother was human. Although she was basically a happy person, she had her problems."

"I know," I say, but I don't really. Yet I have to face the fact she must have. My father isn't easy to live with. I'm finding that out this week.

"Mama was going downhill fast. We all knew it. I think it bothered your mother more than she let on. She kept saying how fragile life is."

The waitress brings our hamburgers, fries, coleslaw, asks if we want anything else. We both shake our heads, and she heads back to the kitchen.

The couple behind us is still arguing. The woman, with gray hair and horn-rimmed glasses, is trying to persuade her husband to buy new furniture.

"So what would she say?" This weird feeling grows inside me—regret mixed with surprise—and not really wanting to know about my mother not being happy.

"She'd just say—" Sandra shakes her head "—she'd say that she wanted your father to do things and he wouldn't."

"What things?" I ask, then hope they weren't sex things. I don't think I could stand to hear that!

"Things like going places. To the movies, out to dinner. Your mother was a doer, you know that. Your dad isn't. So she ended up doing a lot by herself, with me, when I could. I think she was lonely."

"Yeah." A tiny memory moves in, foggy, unformed. My mother asking my father to take her to a Monet art exhibit at the Getty, and my father laughing, asking her why in the hell would he want to go there?

Hurt wells up and I rub my forehead.

"I knew I shouldn't have said anything." Sandra sighs. "But I thought it might give you insight into why your dad is acting the way he is. He had to have known that your mother wasn't all that happy."

"Why didn't she tell me?" I take a bite of my hamburger, but it tastes like cardboard. "I would have listened."

"Because you don't tell your daughter those things about her father. Or at least your mother wouldn't." Sandra begins eating, covers her mouth as she speaks. "This is better than I thought it would be." She looks back to the kitchen. "Kudos to the chef."

The cook, a man in his early forties, waves, smiles.

"Is there anything else?" I don't know why I ask this. I don't want to peer inside my parents' marriage, look at my mother's unhappiness, my father's mistreatment of her.

"Are you sure you want to know?"

In spite of what I feel, I nod.

"Well, she wanted to put together a historical society to save the lighthouse, but she didn't want to do it alone. Jake told her she was crazy. It really hurt her feelings. She had such high hopes."

My mother never told me this, and I feel jealous of Sandra for being so close to her.

"I thought her ideas were really good. We talked about them. I almost had her convinced to do it. And…"

"And?"

"I got the feeling she wanted to, but she was afraid Jake would give her a hard time about it."

A knot in my throat grows, and I feel tears pooling in my eyes. Why the hell didn't she tell me? I push my feelings back, gnaw on my bottom lip

"So maybe that's why your father is doing this. I'd leave him alone. Let him heal this way, let him have a chance of making peace with all this."

CHAPTER 9

I'm standing on the top front porch step, taking in the twilight. Beginning shadows and fading sunlight are mixing with the streetlamp that just came on. My mother loved this time. She told me once the world relaxed, stretched out at twilight. And now I can see what she meant.

Sandra and I finished eating and walked home. The couple behind us were still arguing! And what Sandra told me about my mother is still sinking in. I guess, deep down, I knew my mother struggled with my father, but I didn't want to admit it to myself. Who wants to think of her mother unhappy?

But I've decided to stop interfering in Dad's life. It's obvious he has some guilt and he doesn't want suggestions from me about his project. I'm bothering him more than I'm helping. If he feels guilty about Mom and needs to fix up the lighthouse, then so be it.

I look up the street. Dad is coming down the sidewalk, limping. I go to the end of the walk.

"Are you okay?" I call out.

He pats the air as if to back me off. "Yeah. Fine." As he gets closer, I see he's filthy and his hair is covered with white dust.

"Why are you limping?"

His expression turns sheepish. "Well, remember those stairs you said might be dangerous?"

"What happened?"

"I fell off the third step. Nothing serious. See." He walks forward, winces and rubs his hip.

"Right, nothing serious." I shake my head, feel exhausted and hopeless. "You could have really hurt yourself."

"It was just a couple of steps. Don't worry."

"Dad, don't you understand? You have not been acting like yourself." I study him. He's got bluish circles under his eyes and he looks so tired. "Are you getting any sleep?"

"Yeah. A little. I cleaned out a lot of debris in

the lighthouse today. You should see her now. She's looking better."

"But now you've hurt your hip. You could have broken a bone. You should go to Dr. Van Wagoner, let her check it for you."

"I told you, I'm fine," he says, then grimaces again.

I rub my forehead and tell myself I need to realize he doesn't want me to be a part of his life. I'll be gone soon, out of this, so why bother now? Things between us are never going to change.

"Okay, Dad."

He starts up the steps to the house, stops and turns back. "From today on, I'm planning to work fourteen hours a day. That's what it's going to take to bring her up to code." He takes another step to the porch.

"Dad, wait."

He turns around again. "What?"

"I think I'll go home early. You're really busy now and Christmas is over. I was only going to stay until New Years', anyway."

He looks at me, his expression serious. "If that's what you want to do."

"If I go home, I can get some work done, too Maybe sell a house or two."

"When do you think you'll go?"

"Tomorrow. I'll call the airline tonight, see if I can change my reservation."

"Let me know when you need to go to the airport."

What I want him to say is: "Don't go, stay, we'll go do something, or talk, or *something*," but he doesn't.

"Maybe you should go lie down?"

"Nope, I'm going to shower then head to the library. To save money, I've decided to wire the lighthouse myself."

No smile or laugh. "That's pretty serious work. What about Adam?"

"I'll be okay doing it."

"Like with the stairs?"

"I lost my footing, no big deal."

"What if you had hit your head? You'd still be lying there. For God's sake, Dad, don't you see that?"

He rubs his hip, looks at me, but doesn't say anything. His silence ignites the anger in me.

"All I've done since I've been here is worry about you. I wanted to come home and get to know you."

"We know each other."

"No, we don't! We don't talk. When we do, we fight." Sadness creeps into my throat, my chest.

"We talk, we're talking now," he says, a look of confusion growing on his face.

A memory of my mother surfaces. She's standing between us, her hand touching my father's shoulder. *Oh, Jake, try to understand her, talk to her.*

"Okay!" I say, lifting my hands into the air. "Then talk to me now. Do you feel guilty about Mom? Is that what this lighthouse thing is all about? I'll understand, I promise." I startle myself with the question, but I'm beyond caring.

"I did my best." Dad's eyes narrow a little, then he looks down the street into the growing darkness. "Maybe that wasn't good enough for you."

"I meant—"

He looks back. "Like not calling when you could."

My heart begins to throb and the lump in my throat grows. Here we go.

I take a deep breath. "I just want to know why you are so motivated about the lighthouse, that's all." I know this isn't true. Deep down, I want to lash out and hurt him, make him see me—not be some invisible daughter.

"I forgot something at the lighthouse. I'll be back in a few minutes."

He brushes past me, down the sidewalk, the streetlight highlighting his limp.

"You always leave!" I yell, but he doesn't turn around, and I watch until he disappears.

It's seven-thirty in the morning and I'm walking. I was hoping this would help me get my mind off our argument last night, but it isn't working. I called the airline, but I could only change my reservation to tomorrow.

Now that I've decided I'm leaving, I'm anxious to go home. I keep checking messages, calling the office. I'm not missing a thing. At least, when I get home, I can put in office hours, work on getting more contracts.

A motorcycle drives by, circles, and Adam smiles at me. He pulls up by the sidewalk, shuts off his bike and takes off his helmet. His brown hair is sticking up in places, flattened out in others. For some reason, it looks okay on him.

"How are you?" he asks.

"I'm okay."

"Just okay?"

"No, I'm fine."

"Where you going?"

"The park." I want to go there, say an official goodbye to my mother, since I'm leaving tomorrow.

"Want a ride?" He gestures to the extra helmet on the back seat.

"Me on a motorcycle? I don't think so."

"Why not? The Department of Motor Vehicles thinks I'm safe."

I laugh, nod. "Yeah, like they know what they're doing. Have you seen the people they give driver's licenses to?"

Adam grins, pats his bike. "Oh, come on. Live a little."

"Is this the same bike you bought in Oregon, the *Easy Rider* one?"

"No, I crashed that one a long time ago."

"That's why I think I'll walk."

"Then so will I." He kickstands his bike, straps the helmet on the seat, then looks at me. "That is if you want some company?"

"I don't mind, but aren't you afraid someone will take your motorcycle?"

"Nah."

We begin walking.

"So what's new?" he asks.

"I'm heading home tomorrow." We are close to the park, and I can hear the ocean.

"You're going home so soon?"

"Yeah, I need to get back to Tucson. I've got a lot to do." I gesture to my cell phone that's clipped to my waistband.

"Right."

At the park, we walk through the lighthouse gate, and I notice it doesn't squeak. I try the door, but it's locked. "I guess Dad's not here."

"Probably went for supplies." He looks around. "You know, you've got to give him credit for dedicating himself to this place."

"Yeah, I guess so. I just don't want him to kill himself doing it."

We walk to the bench close by and sit.

"Weather's nice," I say, lifting my face to the sun, feeling the heat on it. I think about how I used to tell my mother goodbye right before I'd leave, and I can almost hear her say, "*I don't want you to go.*" She always said that when I was leaving. My throat grows tight and I can feel tears. I sniff, shake my head, tell them to go away.

"You okay?" Adam is looking at me with concern.

"Yeah, fine. Just thinking. The sun feels good."

"You have a boyfriend in Arizona?"

His question is so direct, I laugh. "No. I haven't had a boyfriend in a long time, well, a serious one in two years."

"I haven't had a girlfriend in a while, either."

"In a dry spell?" I think about how many men I've gone through, how many times I've thought a man was that one special guy, the Prince Charming my mother told me about. And he turned out to be someone I didn't even know.

"Yeah, guess I am. My last girlfriend moved to Minneapolis."

"Why didn't you go with her?"

He looks at me, blinks. "I'm not sure I really cared that much. What about you?"

I hold up my hand, touch my thumb. "Caught one cheating." I grab my index finger. "Another wasn't into me, a few fought too much, one was too bossy…." I stop at my pinkie, realize the pattern in my life. "Maybe I was looking for Mr. Perfect."

"No one is perfect."

"Yeah, I'm finding that out. But there was a really nice guy once." I think about Ian, how much I cared for him. And then I'm surprised when I realize that it's been four years since we broke up. We'd gone together for five. He wanted to get married, I didn't. He thought I shouldn't work so hard, and I interpreted that as being controlling.

"What happened?" Adam leans back, looks up at the lighthouse.

"I was working on being the best Realtor. Now I'm one of my company's top producers. I guess he got tired of waiting for me. And then he moved to New York for a lifetime opportunity."

Adam smiles. "Lifetime opportunities happen every day. We just have to be ready to accept them, to wrap our arms around them and let go."

I turn and face him. He is no one I would ever be attracted to, but I really like him. "*Let go?* Don't you mean hold tight?"

"No, let go. Hold tight and things slip away, like a handful of water." He flattens his left hand, then closes his fingers.

"How do you do it?" I look up at the beautiful sky.

"Do what?" Adam tilts his head back.

"See things in such a different way. My mother used to do that, too."

He stands, looks around. "I just let myself. It's not a trick. You have to believe, that's all."

"Believe in what?"

"Believe that life can be good. That the little things in life make us who we are, feel alive. That each day is a gift we shouldn't waste."

"It's hard for me to believe anything like that, especially now. If you had known my mother…if anyone needed to live it was her. She loved life." I look at the lighthouse. "She even loved that." I gesture toward the building.

"There's a plan, we just don't know what it is," he says.

"What *plan?*" I stand, get ready to walk back if Adam is going to start talking about religion.

"Everybody has a path. Remember when I first

saw you in the café'? I believe I was supposed to be there. I think you needed someone to talk to, give you some encouragement. And maybe we even have another connection we don't even know about."

I hold very still. "What kind of plan would take my mother away? She was a good person. Look at my dad, how he is now—lonely, brokenhearted."

"Maybe there's a reason, something needed to happen and the only way for it to take place was that your mother had to die."

When he says that last word, I want to slap him.

"Oh, that's just bullshit! What plan could there be for my mother's death?"

"You have to figure it out. My uncle used to say our lives are choreographed, we're just too taken with living to realize it."

"What kind of a stupid plan is that?"

"There are things out there—" he gazes up at the sky, squints "—things…we can't understand, but they're miracles."

I feel a mixture of anger and sadness. "I don't want to believe that a miracle took my mother. It's better if it was a stupid accident!"

Adam moves closer and puts his hand on my shoulder. I can feel his warmth against my skin. He smiles.

"I didn't mean to make you feel sad. Honest."

He smiles with such innocence I forgive him.

"It's just you might want to think about opening up to new possibilities about your mother. Relax, something will come to you."

He leans forward and I pull back. I don't want him to kiss me, for God's sake! He is quicker than I am, and he gives me a little brotherly kiss on my forehead. Then he's out of my space.

"Christine, I like you, but not in that way. I just want to be your friend, that's all."

I laugh.

"What's funny?"

"You. I was just thinking the same thing."

"Maybe that's what you need, humor."

"Maybe."

"Just think about what I said. You'll find something to inspire you. Nothing in this world is an accident."

CHAPTER 10

My father and his friend Chet walk up to the park bench where Adam and I are sitting. Dad isn't limping and this makes me feel relieved. He's carrying two paint cans by their thin wire handles.

I introduce Adam to Chet.

"Your hip doesn't hurt?" I ask Dad.

"I'm fine. It was just a little bump." He turns to Chet, smiles. "This kid worries about everything. A little fall last night and she acts as if I took a header off the top of the lighthouse."

"My kids are the same." Chet nods to me. "It's nice you could come home to see your father for Christmas."

"It is?" I ask, and look at the paint cans, notice the lids are splashed with a sugary white.

Dad sets them on the ground. "I'm not going to

paint for a while, but these were on special, so I grabbed them. Any money I can save is worth it."

"I think you're going to need a lot more paint than two cans." I imagine him on a ladder, falling, me racing toward him, arms out—the entire scenario like a cartoon.

"Yeah, the place needs painting inside and out."

"Where are you going to start?" Adam asks.

"Inside's the priority. For the outside I'll need big ladders, scaffolding."

"Oh, God," I say. Everyone turns and looks at me, and I laugh to cover up what I let slip out.

"Don't worry, I'm going to help him," Chet says. He's been Dad's friend for as long as I can remember, and he's a nice guy. He's divorced, and Mom used to invite him for dinner a lot.

"How's the wiring coming?" Adam asks.

"Picked up some electrical books from the library, but I have to wait for the parts," Dad says.

"I might be able to help you with that." Adam smiles, and my heart melts a little. I wouldn't have to worry so much if Adam were helping him.

"Don't think I'll have a problem."

Adam crosses his arms. "Can you get a discount

on parts? Plus I'll check your work. That way when the lighthouse is inspected, you'll be sure to pass."

Dad studies him for a moment, looks at Chet. "This is a nice kid. You sure you have time?"

"Yeah, wouldn't offer if I didn't."

"Great, I'll get in touch." Dad picks up the paint, and he and Chet walk to the lighthouse, then disappear behind it.

"At times," I say, "everything seems okay with him. You know, I'm just not used to worrying about him. My mother was always here to do that."

"He'll be okay. I'll help him with the wiring, keep him out of trouble. Might be interesting."

I turn my attention to the sky, breathe deeply for a few moments, remind myself that I'll be home tomorrow, working, maybe showing a house, writing a contract soon, hopefully not consumed with worry.

"When do you think you'll come back?" Adam asks.

I look at him. "Well, this trip hasn't been too successful. I might not come back." I surprise myself but know it's true. I study the trees, the lighthouse, lean back and drink in a little air in honor of my mom.

"Although I'll miss this. It reminds me so much of my mother."

"How about your dad?"

"I won't miss fighting with him. I expected to come home and be friends. That was pretty stupid, wasn't it?"

"Not really. I admire that."

I don't tell Adam how I wish I could go back to the day before my mother died, call her, say something that would keep her off the freeway, and then explain how lucky I was to have her in my life.

"We all have regrets," Adam says.

"What?" I look at him.

"Your expression seems so regretful."

"You don't seem like you have any regrets."

"I wish I had known you in high school. We could have been friends. I needed friends back then." He smiles and so do I.

"Well, we're friends now. Thanks for offering to help Dad." I put my hand on his shoulder and pat him a little.

"He's an okay guy."

"We've never found common ground. Actually, I don't think he likes me very much."

Adam's eyes narrow and he turns his head, like he's trying to figure out what I've just said. "You believe that?"

"Yes. I was a screwup for a long time. Dad likes perfect. And we never agree on anything."

"Guys have funny ways of showing they care. They don't know how to work on relationships. They kind of let them happen. Just relax and it'll unfold."

"I leave tomorrow. Not much unfolding time left."

"Maybe you should stay."

I laugh. "No, I can't. The housing market really pops after Christmas. People come down from the east to escape the cold." But the real reason I want to go home early is to avoid thinking about my mother all the time and arguing with my dad.

I look at the lighthouse, imagine my father walking around it after I leave, all alone. "Just do me a favor, if you can. When you're working on the electricals, look after him."

I take another Santa off the Christmas tree, wrap it in tissue and place the ornament in the box on the hardwood floor. Warm sunshine fills the room. My mother used to sit here, on the couch in the afternoons, drinking tea and listening to Bach.

Before Adam and I left the park this morning, he gave my father his card, told him he was going to walk me home, get his motorcycle, then he'd be back. At our front door, he shook my hand, and I thanked him for listening to me, for helping.

I pull another red-and-white Santa off the fake tree, wrap it in the wrinkled tissue. There is a faint hint of my mother's perfume, Obsession, on the tissue, and I bring the wrapped Santa to my nose, sniff, then place it alongside the others in the box. A memory: my mother and I talking about Christmas decorations. Last year, I called when she was putting the ornaments away. She seemed down, so I told her she should leave the Christmas lights up all year.

She explained that leaving the lights up would take away the magic for next year.

I look at the fake tree, the huge red lights. *Some magic.* I bring my hands to the sides of my face and breathe in, think about this morning with Adam. Is he right about letting things unfold, that maybe someday I'll have a relationship with my father?

Three wrapped Santas later, I hear the back door

open, close. Instead of turning around, I carefully take another ornament and nestle it in tissue.

"Hi, honey."

I turn, smile, sweep back memories and worries as if they were fall leaves littering a porch.

"Thought I'd take down the tree for you. That way you won't have to do it. You have enough work with the lighthouse."

"Thanks. I was planning on leaving the tree up till New Year's, but since you're going, there's not much point."

"Did you and Chet get a lot done?"

"Yeah. I also talked to Adam about the electricals. He's going to draw up a plan, after he inspects the place."

I nod, feel relief. I take another Santa and, for the first time, notice how light the decoration is. I always thought they were heavy. I bounce it in my hand. "These are really delicate."

Dad walks over. "Your mother really liked them."

"Aren't there more?" I gesture to the small box.

"Two boxes in the garage. Last week I tried not to break any but I cracked two."

"You did a good job with the tree." I force myself to smile. "Christmas was nice. You want me to put the tree in the garage?"

"Sure, for next year."

I think about Dad standing here, putting up the tree by himself, my mother's memory probably saturating his every thought.

"Maybe you should leave the tree up till New Year's." I reach down, pick up a wrapped Santa, unwrap it.

"Nah, it's best it comes down. I appreciate the help."

Scented tissue floats to the carpet.

Dad pulls an ornament off, studies it. "I didn't want your mother to buy these. We had a little argument about them. I thought she spent too much. I was always worried about money."

I look at him. "She loved these ornaments. I'm glad she got them, enjoyed them."

Dad moves back to his chair but doesn't sit. "I never liked Christmas until I met her. Thought it was a bunch of bullshit."

"You never liked it after, either."

He laughs, walks back to the tree, narrowing the space between us.

"My mother, your grandmother, hated Christmas. It was always a mess with her when Christmas rolled around. She was a boozer. She'd get drunk, make a scene no matter where we were. The only place she behaved was in church."

Dad had never talked about his mother, and I never knew her.

He takes a deep breath, sighs.

"I tried to go along with the Christmas things your mother wanted even though it wasn't me. I realized little by little that's what you do when you plan to be with someone for a lifetime."

"I'm sure Mom—"

"She tried to teach me a lot about life, what was important to her. Some things I learned, some I didn't."

I look at the ornament lying in my hand, the glistening white and red. I have no idea where this set came from, why she liked them so much. "Where did Mom get these?"

"Bought them in a dime store out in Torrance that was going out of business. She found the sales ad in the newspaper, then filled up the car trunk. She loved a bargain. She bought extras. In case some broke, we'd still have enough for years to come."

"For future Christmases."

"Yeah. For the future."

Jake faced the lighthouse. Against the night sky it looked eerie, reminding him of an odd-shaped turret from a castle.

The look on Christine's face when he told her he hadn't wanted Dorothy to buy the Christmas tree ornaments was still bothering him. Why had he even said anything? What went on between him and his wife was his business, not anyone else's, not even his daughter's.

God, he missed Dorothy. She was the one who loved Christine, made it right with her when he was grouchy or too demanding. Now there was no one to do that. He wasn't a good father, not at all, and Dorothy had struggled so hard with that fact. A dull ache pulsed through his body, stopped at his chest, right above his heart. Christine was going home tomorrow. He'd work at being nice till then so she'd leave with a good feeling.

He felt resolved and walked around the lighthouse, keyed the lock and walked into the circular room. Darkness surrounded him. He needed to be in Dorothy's presence for just a moment. Was it like this for addicts, needing a fix—half-crazy wanting it?

Jake closed his eyes. His energy was waning and turning into exhaustion. How in the hell was he going to get all this work done? He should go home, sleep and regenerate, get a fresh start tomorrow. He didn't want to become the laughingstock of the town. Holding his life together until the lighthouse was finished had to be his priority.

Jake walked out the door, turned and set the padlock. The bolt clunked into place, and he headed through the gate.

Sandra and I are sitting in, according to Sandra, the only decent bar in San Pedro—the Crab Catcher. It's a typical beach hangout, complete with a stuffed marlin hanging over the beer taps. Someone has strung red Christmas lights around the top of the bar, put a Santa hat on the marlin, and really, it actually looks festive. I'm more relaxed than I have been in days, knowing I'm leaving tomorrow. So I'm ready for a few laughs.

Adam called me tonight, after Dad left for his walk, and asked if I felt like going for a drink. I wanted to get out of the house so I accepted, then called Sandra and invited her to come along, explaining I was going to meet Adam.

"I'm glad you asked me," Sandra says now, taking a big sip of her Manhattan. "I need to go out more. Four walls can start to push in on a person."

I nod, familiar with the feeling from living in Tucson, sitting in my condo night after night, working on contracts and talking on the phone to clients.

We are sitting in a cushy booth in the back of the bar. "Little Deuce Coup" begins playing on the jukebox and we both bob our heads in time with the music.

She holds up her drink. "I really need *this* more than anything."

"So do I." I lick margarita salt from my lips. Sandra drove so I figure I'm having more than one margarita. She came to get me right after work and didn't change her clothes. She looks pretty in her light blue sweater, pearls and black skirt.

I smile.

"What?"

"You look cute with your pearls, you know, your *office attire*."

"Right. If it's one thing I'm not, it's *cute*, but—" she smooths her skirt "—thanks. Better than my sweats, don't you think?"

"I like your sweats. Did you see your mom today?"

"Yeah, I went on my lunch hour." She shakes her head.

"What?"

"I don't want to bring you down, too."

"You won't," I say, but I'm not sure this is true. I've been thinking about Josephine a lot lately. And the thoughts are not good.

"She's losing more memory by the hour. Today she didn't even know where her bed was. It's like someone comes in when she's sleeping, dips into her brain and takes out another scoop."

The waitress brings chips and salsa, but neither of us takes any.

"But it's good you can check on her, make sure she's being taken care of."

Sandra nods. "Yeah, that's something. Lose your mind, but you have your daughter checking on you, who, by the way, you don't know from the janitor. That's one hell of a consolation prize for being a nice person." She smiles a little. "Sorry I'm so cynical, but sometimes I just don't get this life."

"I know *that* feeling. How do you do what you're doing? Keep going on. I think I'd have trouble with it."

"Like I have a choice. One foot in front of the other, baby. No one knows how tough it is unless they've done it. There are times I want to scream. And I feel like all I'm going to have left are these terrible memories." She shakes her head. "Damn."

"Maybe someday you'll remember the good times, the way she really was. The vibrant person she always was."

"I hope so." Sandra's expression is a study in sadness.

The last time I saw my mother, she was taking down the tree. It was two years ago. She was smiling, talking about what a wonderful time she had that year. Sometimes there is a consolation prize.

"You've helped me," Sandra says.

I laugh. "How's that?"

"With you here, I've been thinking more about how my mother used to be. The good memories are coming back. Can't you stay a little longer?"

"Sorry, I need to go back. I've got listings up the wazoo, open houses planned, showings." These things aren't going to be happening until after New Year's, but I don't want to tell her why I'm really going. Sandra's got enough to deal with.

"I was just hoping. You know, maybe with more time, you'd get closer to your dad."

"I'm resolved that's not going to happen. The rift between us is as big as the Grand Canyon."

"Isn't it weird that we're worried about our parents? We're probably sounding like the way our parents did when we were younger."

"'Weird' doesn't begin to describe it," I say.

Sandra smiles. "Do you miss Pedro at all?"

I nod, take a sip of my margarita. "I'm beginning to miss it a lot. Tucson's okay, but I'm not really a desert girl. I guess I've got ocean water in my veins, always will. And I'm so busy with work, I don't have time to enjoy Tucson."

I look over Sandra's shoulder, see Adam walk through the door. He's smiling as usual. He looks so comfortable in his own skin.

"There's Adam," I say, and wave him over.

"Oh, God, are you sure I'm not butting in, you know, you might get something going with him."

"We're just acquaintances. I'm definitely not interested in him," I whisper. "He's just a nice guy."

When he gets to the table, I introduce them. He sits next to me, across from Sandra, and looks at her intently. "I remember you from high school. Yeah, I do."

"Really?" Sandra lifts a brow. I've seen this look before, a long time ago, and it's not a good sign.

"Mostly I remember your red hair." Adam gestures toward her. "I always thought it was pretty. Still is."

Sandra doesn't say anything, and my stomach drops. Driving over here, I started worrying they might not like each other. This has happened before. I've introduced friends to friends thinking they'd get along, but it turned into disasters.

Sandra shifts, looks at me, raises her eyebrow again.

"So, Adam, did you go to the lighthouse today?" I ask, trying to fill up the silent space.

"Yeah, your dad's doing a lot of work."

"Too much, probably."

"He seems okay. The place is certainly interesting."

Sandra takes a big swig of her drink, stares past the bar, then looks at me. "Tine, I had an idea."

"What's that?"

"I was thinking, maybe I could help your dad with the lighthouse. I need the exercise, and it could be fun. I haven't pounded a nail in a long time, but I like the idea of construction work. On the weekends, I don't do much after I check on Mama. I might be of some help to Jake."

"Great idea," Adam says. "I'm helping him with the electricals."

"Don't you have enough to do? With your mom and everything?" I ask.

"Not really. Of course, I don't know anything about construction, but I could learn, and when I'm not with Mama, the work might help me to not worry."

"Busy hands, silent mind," Adam says.

"What?" Sandra says, squinting at him.

"If you keep busy, it helps to silence the mind. A tenet in Buddhism."

"Oh" is all Sandra says.

Adam looks around the bar. And Sandra rolls her eyes at me.

"I could help Jake with the easy lifting projects," Sandra says.

"Easy *listening?*" Adam laughs, bringing his attention back to us. Sandra gives him a weird look.

"No, I said easy *lifting.*"

"Oh, yeah."

I take a big swig of my drink. This isn't how I thought this would go. And I'm not so excited about Sandra helping my father. I can't imagine Dad saying okay to her help, and for some stupid reason, I feel a little jealous.

The waitress comes over, takes Adam's drink order. Sandra leans forward, elbows on the table, smiles.

"So what do you think? Good idea?"

I shake my head, feel a little light-headed from drinking my margarita so fast.

"What? No?" Sandra asks.

"You know how he is. I'm not sure he'll let anyone help, except Chet, maybe Adam because he needs someone who knows electrical work."

We sit for a moment, listening to the music, until the waitress brings Adam's beer and he pays her. He takes a drink, looks at both of us.

"I decided to donate my time and electrical supplies to the lighthouse. I haven't told your father yet, but that's what I'm going to do. It's for a good cause, to preserve history."

"Good luck. He's pretty independent," I say.

"He's under the gun time-wise, and I figure with money, too. He won't say no, he's too smart."

"Well, maybe. Tomorrow before I leave, I'll ask him if you can help, Sandra," I say, squeezing her hand and feeling bad for being a little cranky. "It's nice of you to offer. I'll feel better if you both keep an eye on him for me."

I pick up my drink, clink it against Sandra's Manhattan glass and then Adam's beer bottle. "Here's to both of you, safe travel, and me, selling a boatload of houses."

CHAPTER 11

I'm in the driveway by my father's car, enveloped in early morning fog. I came out for some fresh air in hopes of getting rid of my headache before I start packing. I drank way too much last night. I have the margarita flu, but I don't care. After Adam and Sandra got comfortable, we had fun talking.

Instead of pulling in the garage, Dad left the Volvo in the driveway, parked at a weird angle. I made the mistake of looking inside. It's a mess. I know it's a small thing, a messy car, but my father has always kept his cars immaculate. Every week he'd hook up the hose and wash his car with a special soap that wouldn't dull the paint. Then, when he finished, he'd polish off the water beads with a chamois. After that, he'd open all the doors like wings and rub Armor All on the dash.

When I was a kid, I tried to help. Sometimes

he'd let me dry the hood a little, until he got impatient and said I was too slow.

I visor my eyes, press my hand against the back window again and notice the dome light is on. At least twenty books with yellow library stickers are stacked on the back seat. Three crumpled sacks from McDonald's are on the floor and the doors are unlocked.

"God," I whisper.

"Morning," Dad says. I look over toward the house. He's standing on the porch. "What are you doing?"

"Trying to get rid of a headache. Did you know your car's unlocked and the inside light is on?"

"Door's probably ajar."

I open the back door, shut it, and the light goes off. "Why didn't you put your car in the garage?"

"Guess I'm getting lazy." He opens the kitchen door and walks back into the house. I go inside, find him by the sink.

"If I had time I'd clean out your car," I say.

"Don't worry about the car. I'll get to it later."

"Remember how you'd wash your car and Mom's every week?" I gesture to the backyard.

"Yeah. I was pretty fanatical about it. Now I've got the lighthouse to worry about. What time did you come home last night?"

"We closed the bar." I start toward the dining room, turn around. "I almost forgot. Sandra volunteered to help you with the lighthouse. You should take her up on it."

He just stares at me.

"It's going to take a long time to do all the renovating if you do everything yourself."

"That might work."

I close the space between us, put my hand on his arm. "Sandra said she needs the exercise, and Adam is really interested in the place, not just the electrical work, he wants to donate his time and the materials."

He nods, and my heart relaxes a little. "They can help me if they want, but you know how that goes."

"No, I don't."

"Volunteers don't show up, they argue. If I hire people, then if that stuff starts, I can fire them."

"Hiring people is good, I guess. Can you afford it?"

Dad shrugs. "Not really. I'd better take a shower, get ready to drive you to the airport."

* * *

I close my suitcase, then check my room to make sure I have everything. I hear the kitchen door open then close, so I pop up my roller-bag handle and squeak down the hall, past the bathroom. I don't look in. I don't want to see my mother's makeup mirror right before I leave.

"I'm ready," I say, walking into the kitchen.

Dad's standing by the sink with his hands on the counter.

"I hope I didn't forget anything." I move my suitcase a little, close my eyes against the ache in my head.

"Go back and check."

"I did just a minute ago."

"Then we'd better hit the road. Let me have your bag."

"I can get it."

He takes the handle, anyway, and waves me forward. I go to the back door, make the mistake of looking back into the kitchen. Sunlight soaks the walls, the table and chairs with crystal light. A memory descends, sits with my headache—my mother and I looking in her makeup mirror—the bathroom full of bright light. She rubs lotion on my sunburned cheek. I feel her cool touch on my skin, look in the mirror and see our faces close together.

You stayed out too long trying to help Daddy. He loves you, Chrissy, but he has no patience.

"We'd better get a move on it."

Dad's words pull me back to the kitchen.

"Just a minute," I say.

"We need to leave."

"I forgot something."

Dad looks at his watch and then the sunflower clock. "If traffic is bad—"

"I'll hurry." I sprint to the dining room, through the living room and down the hall. When I get to the bathroom, I see my mother's makeup mirror, know it has to go with me. I unplug it and bring it close to my chest. Then I pick up her perfume bottle.

"I'm sorry," I say when I walk back into the kitchen, with the mirror cord trailing behind me. "Do you mind if I take these?" I hold up the mirror, the Obsession.

"You want both?"

"I'd like them."

"Will they fit in your suitcase?"

"I think so." I kneel, wind up the cord, then unzip my suitcase and nestle the mirror against a two-week-old *People* magazine and my pajamas.

"We need to get a move on."

I close my bag, stand and realize I forgot to put the perfume in my suitcase. I'll put it in my purse when I get settled in the car.

"I'm ready." I feel better and walk out the door first. We are silent as he opens the trunk, puts my suitcase in. Dad holds the car door and I climb in. I don't look back, don't want to feel like dirt because I'm going home early and probably won't come back for a very long time.

Dad settles behind the wheel, turns the key.

A *tat-tat-tat* sound. He tries again. The same sound, then nothing.

"The battery's dead," he says.

I look at the dome light. A rawness roars through my body. I don't want to go through leaving the house again.

"Sandra's not home so she can't drive me. I guess I'll have to call a cab."

"Just wait a minute," Dad says, and tries to start

the car again, but it's dead. I open the car door and run across the yard. A whack—Dad slamming his door—singes the air.

I twist the doorknob. The house is locked.

"Let me get the door." Dad keys the door, opens it, and I rush to the phone. I place the Obsession bottle on the counter, find the phone book and begin looking for the taxi listings. Dad sighs and I look over at him. Sun highlights his gray hair and lined face.

"Call now or you won't make your flight."

I turn back too quickly, knock the perfume bottle off the counter and it somersaults to the floor. When it hits the tile, glass smashes, clattering, glittery.

And then in the silence, my mother's scent encircles us.

"Oh, God, I'm sorry. I don't know how I did that."

Dad crosses the kitchen, kneels down next to the mess and just stares at it.

"It was her last bottle. She wanted me to buy her another and I forgot," he says.

"I'm sorry. I was in a hurry."

He looks up at me as if he's lost.

"Are you okay?" I kneel beside him, expecting him to brush me away, but he doesn't. I place my hand on his shoulder—find he's trembling.

He closes his eyes.

"Dad?"

"I never thought this would happen."

"I'm so sorry I dropped the perfume."

"It's not that." He picks up a tiny piece of glass. "It feels like she's right here, but she isn't."

"I know. Since I've been here, I can't stop thinking about her." Words tumble together, rush out. "I was in the bathroom the other night, and I swear I expected to see her standing by the door. And sometimes, when I walked into the kitchen, I had this quick moment where I thought she would be sitting at the table in the same place she always sat."

I look at Dad. His jaw tightens and I can tell he's trying not to cry.

"I've been feeling like she's closer," he whispers.

"Really?" My heart begins to hurt—throb—because I've never seen my father so close to breaking down. Even at the funeral he remained stoic, his expression frozen.

"Sometimes I feel like she's right here." He looks down at the broken bottle, picks up another perfume-soaked piece of glass.

"I'll clean that up, Dad."

"No, I'll do it. Call a cab!"

I jump up as if I'm eight in response to his sharp words. Why does he always do this? I'm glad I'll be gone soon.

I go to the phone, flip through the phone book, which has been in the same place for years. I take a deep breath, to tamp down my anger. I watch as Dad reaches for another piece of glass under the table, loses his balance and stretches his hand out to catch himself.

"Damn it!"

"What?"

He leans back and a drop of blood falls into the perfume puddle, expands and turns sunrise pink.

"Jesus." He gets up, goes to the sink, pulls a paper towel off the roll. Red begins to seep onto white.

"How bad is it?" I cross the kitchen, stand near him.

"I don't know."

I touch his hand, feel the warmth of his skin. "Let me see. You're bleeding."

"It's fine. Go call your cab."

I look at the paper towel, see more blood than I've seen in a long time. My heart starts beating faster. "It isn't fine."

"It'll stop. I'm putting pressure on it."

"Let me see it!" I'm so tired and frustrated with this game we've been playing most of our lives.

He holds out his hand, palm up. More blood. I take the paper towel, dab at it, see a V-shaped gash cut into the heel of his hand, and I feel a little weak.

"Oh, God."

"It's fine."

"I think you need stitches."

Dad takes the paper towel, presses it against the cut. "It's okay, call your cab."

"You need to see the doctor. What are you going to do, walk around with this open wound? You won't be able to get any work done in the lighthouse."

Dad looks at me. "Maybe you're right."

"I know I'm right. Where's the closest urgent care?"

"I don't know."

"You don't know?"

"Your mother always took care of stuff like that."

I go to the phone book, find a place up on Western Avenue, then realize we don't have a way to get there. I look over at Dad. He's sitting at the table with his head down, paper towel pressed against his hand. I could call Sandra, but she's at work and I don't want to disturb her. Then I think of Adam. He might not mind taking us.

"Adam will come get us if he's not busy."

"Don't call him."

"And what are we supposed to do?" My headache is still pounding. I look through my purse, dig out Adam's card and two soft blue Aleves. I dial the number. He answers and I explain what happened, about the car, my father's hand. Without hesitation, he tells me he'll be over in a few minutes.

I cross the room, pop the pills into my mouth, wash them down, then sit by Dad. "You okay?"

"Yeah." He pulls the paper towel away as if to show me.

The cut has stopped bleeding, but without the blood it looks deep, angry. "Does it hurt?"

He shakes his head.

"Adam will be here in a few minutes."

"You should go to the airport. I'll take care of this."

"No" is all I say.

After I get the broom and start sweeping, I think about missing my flight, don't really care because I feel so sorry for my father. I sweep the glass and the brown tear-shaped lid into the dustpan, then take it out to the large garbage can by the garage. When I come back into the house, Dad is still sitting at the table.

"Well, that's cleaned up." I take a deep breath. The scent of my mother's perfume has permeated the room.

"Thanks."

I mop up the rest of the perfume and tiny grains of glass with a wad of paper towels, then sit down across from him. "You want me to get you something?"

"No."

A tiny rainbow from the crystal bear Mom placed on the windowsill dances on the wall across from us. One time, I asked her why the rainbow wasn't always there.

If you want it to be there, pretend it is.

I laugh.

"What?"

"That little bear over there." I gesture to the window. "It always throws a rainbow on the wall in the mornings. I'd forgotten about it till now."

Dad turns around, looks at it. "I never noticed. Or maybe I forgot."

"When I was a kid, one time I asked Mom why the rainbow wasn't always on the wall."

"What did she say?"

"You know her. She didn't explain the dynamics of light through crystal. She told me if I wanted the rainbow on the wall all the time, I should pretend it was there."

Dad looks at his hand, then me. "Pretend, huh?"

"What would you have told me?"

"That the sunlight refracts through the glass, and it's like a rainbow in the sky—light refracting through water." He looks at his hand again. "But right now I'd tell you to pretend."

Adam and I are sitting in the sparse, poorly decorated Western Avenue Urgent Care waiting room. The receptionist just took Dad back to the examining room. I look at my watch and sigh.

"Did you miss your plane?"

"Yeah, about an hour ago."

"There are other planes. You want to use my cell?" He digs in his pocket, tries to hand me his phone.

"No. I have mine." I pull it out, look to see if I have any messages. There are none. "I'll wait till I get Dad situated, then I'll call. I can leave after that."

"What's wrong with his car?"

"Wouldn't start. He left the door ajar, the light was on all night."

"Probably the battery."

I shrug. "He's been leaving his car out in the driveway and it looks like hell. He never did that before. I don't know anymore." I stand up, walk across the reception area, grab a battered *Better Homes and Gardens* and sit down. "I was feeling so relieved I was going home."

"Maybe you better think about staying."

I look at Adam. "I can't stay. I have work, my clients. Even if I stay another day, what difference is it going to make?" I point to the door my father has just walked through.

"You never know. One second can change someone's life forever."

"Tell me about it."

I shake my head, know this situation is never going to be different.

"A few more days wouldn't end the world." Adam smiles.

I think about my office where I work too much, my lonely condo. When I'm completely honest with myself, I realize I don't even like Tucson.

"I have a job, my clients," I say again as if to convince myself.

"San Pedro real estate market is booming, too," he says as he raises his eyebrows. "Plus your father's here."

"And we don't get along."

"Like I said, nothing stays the same."

I nod, flip through the magazine for a few moments. Adam is looking straight ahead, and I bump his left shoulder with my right. He shifts a little, smiles.

"Thanks for bringing us here, and for staying. You have a hangover?"

"No, you?"

"Yeah, a four-margarita hangover. So you think I should stay a little longer?" I guess I asked this because I need to see my life from someone else's perspective. I feel so torn.

"When we were driving over here, Jake's main concern was the lighthouse, whether he can work on it with his hand like it is. You said he's acting different. Maybe you need to keep an eye on him. He seems lonely. You only get one father."

"He doesn't want me to stay. I feel like I'm in the way."

"That's not what he told me at the lighthouse when I talked to him about the electrical work."

"Really?"

"He said he was glad you came to visit, happy for the company. He was probably lonely before and didn't even realize it."

"Oh, he was just saying that. We aren't close. I've never done what he's wanted."

"Who has when it comes to their parents? I was talking to Sandra this morning, and she told me your dad mentioned he was glad you were coming home."

"You were talking to Sandra *this* morning?" I

know my expression has turned to shock. I smile to hide it.

"Yeah, on the phone. I called the hospice."

"You called her?"

"Yeah. I wanted to encourage her about working on the lighthouse. It's a great idea."

"That was nice of you. You know, I was jealous when I first heard her idea because I can't be here to help."

"That's understandable. I was thinking about asking her out. Think she'd go?"

His question stuns me. They didn't seem to click at the Crab Catcher. Maybe Adam didn't realize this.

"I'm not sure. She's pretty busy."

"She was friendly on the phone. She needs to have some fun."

"Maybe. But don't be disappointed if she doesn't accept. That's just her."

He nods. "I'll give it a try."

My stomach knots a little. Adam is so nice, I don't want him to get his feelings hurt. "I'm not sure she dates."

"Right."

I flip through the magazine some more, put it back on the table, sit beside Adam again and think about staying a few more days.

"You know with my father, it's just so weird. I mean—" I wave my hand "—trying to help him, it's hard. I feel like I'm interfering. But then, I feel like I should be here for him, that my mom would want me to help him, no matter what."

"Just stick around and be here for him. Don't try so hard. You don't have to change him. The situation might change on its own."

"Maybe," I say, but I don't believe this for one moment.

CHAPTER 12

"You aren't going home?" Dad asks.

We are standing in the kitchen by the sink. The doctor told Dad not to cover his ten stitches. I'm looking at them, and they remind me of a Frankenstein movie I saw when I was a kid. He also got a tetanus shot. I was happy about that because of all the work he's doing on the lighthouse.

"Do you care if I stay?" I ask, feeling like such an interloper.

"No, but I thought you wanted to go home?"

"I was planning on staying until New Year's, anyway. I called the office this morning when you were getting stitched up. It's still slow, and if something pops, I have arrangements in place for a colleague to look after my listings."

I cross the room, sit at the kitchen table, and he sits across from me. "Realtors do this all the time.

It's no problem." This is only partly true. No one will take care of my clients like I would, but after talking to Adam at the urgent care, I realize I should stay for a few more days and make sure my father is okay. And this feels so weird. I know I should leave, but I don't want to. Maybe I'm using my father for an excuse.

"How long are you staying?"

"Just a few days, until your hand feels better. Don't forget, my original plan was to stay till New Year's. I can help you around the house, maybe cook a little."

Dad studies his hand. "Thought you said you couldn't cook."

"I can't, but I can read. I'll read Mom's cookbook and try a few things. I miss her cooking, the favorites she always made."

He looks at his hand and then me. "I wish I hadn't done this. Then you could go on with your life. You wouldn't have to be troubled with me."

"It's…you're no trouble. I don't mind, really. Does your hand hurt?"

"I just don't want anyone to feel like they have to babysit me."

"Dad, I miss Pedro, too. And I've been in real estate for a while. I know the business. I have agent friends, plenty of money. It's no big deal. Trust me, if something happens, another agent can handle the paperwork, or I can be home in a few hours."

"You shouldn't have to lose business because of me. I'm proud of what you've done."

"You are?" I sit very still and think about what he just said. I've never known my father to be proud of me for anything.

"Yeah. You've worked hard and make a good living for yourself."

Silence sits between us while I digest what he's said.

"So you're going to stay?" he finally asks.

I study his face for a moment. He looks so exhausted. I know Mom wouldn't want me to leave.

"I'll stay for a few more days, like originally planned. Then I'll get out of your hair. I like it here. I really don't want to go home yet." I tell the small fib.

"I'll be busy with the lighthouse."

"That's fine. I'll just do some things around here. And maybe I can help you."

He starts to push his chair back, but I touch his arm and he stops.

"I want to stay. It's not just because of you. I didn't realize how much I miss Pedro, Mom, all of it. I want to be here."

He squints as if he's really listening, not thinking about going down to the park.

"I think you're making a mistake. You should get on with your life. You can't do it here." He gets up, walks to the kitchen door and looks back. "I never want to be a burden to anyone."

"I don't feel like that," I say, yet I do. It would be so much easier to go home, work, do what I know, forget the memories, and not miss my mother so much.

He shakes his head. "Never wanted to be trouble to anyone." And a moment later he leaves.

"Yeah, I'm back to my original plan of staying till New Year's. I was all set to go back, too. Bags packed, out the door. I almost made it," I tell Sandra with a laugh.

She and I are sitting in her living room, on the couch, our legs pulled up under us. The couch is as comfortable as I remember, and it feels like old times, when we were kids. Except now we're talking about our parents instead of gossiping about other girls or boys.

"I'm glad you're staying. You can go back in a few days when your dad is better. What's a few days?"

"Sometimes, honey, a lifetime. The real question is, will he be better in a few days? He wasn't exactly excited about you helping him, either. But maybe he'll change his mind." I run my fingers through my hair. "Or probably he won't."

"So Adam took you to the hospital?" she asks.

"The Doc in the Box up on Western. I thought about calling you but didn't want to bother you at work."

"Call me anytime. Don't be silly."

"I know, but Adam came right over. He sat with me in the waiting room while Dad was getting stitched up. He was the one who made me start thinking I should delay my leaving. He listens really well." I smile.

"He is a nice guy," Sandra says, smiling a different kind of smile, but one I remember from high school.

"God, with all the crap going on I forgot." I tap my forehead.

"What?"

"I feel stupid telling you this, like we're back in high school, but Adam wants to ask you out, to dinner or something. I told him you weren't into dating, that you were too busy. You know, to discourage him, but he said he was going to do it, anyway. Sorry."

"Great."

"What?" She's grinning at me. "Now I'm confused. I didn't think you even liked him."

"He's okay. You know, he called me this morning and encouraged me about working at the lighthouse. We got to talking about my mother and he was really sympathetic. Asked questions. I thought that was nice of him. I was in a pissy mood last night at the Crab Catcher, worried about everything. He's very easy to talk to."

"You want to date him?"

"Maybe. I'm sick of sitting in this house all the time."

"Well, he is a nice guy."

Sandra laughs. "Now, this really sounds like high school."

"I didn't think he was your type."

"Hey, I'm forty-five, I don't have a *type*. He's a good guy and I think, if I could relax, we might have fun. It doesn't have to be anything serious. That's all I'm looking for now. Plus he's handy around the house. What more could a girl ask for when you live in a seventy-five-year-old house?" She laughs and so do I.

"Well, when you put it that way…"

"Too late, he's mine. You know, Tine, think about this. What guy would sit in an urgent care with someone he barely knows for more than ten minutes?"

"Not many."

"What guy would give you advice about your dad? Offer to help with that screwed-up lighthouse?"

"True."

"With all my mother's health problems, I've come to realize being picky about men just *ain't* such a good idea."

"I guess I've been a little picky, too."

"Maybe, a little. Haven't we all? I just know waiting for Mr. Dreamboat isn't going to work for me anymore. I'm taking care of my mother, my job's stressful. I need fun and a low-maintenance guy."

"I wish I could be like you."

"Overweight and cranky?" Sandra shakes her head a little.

"No, accept that I might have to help my father. Just this little bit has me crazy. I don't like being a parent to him, worrying, trying to make him do things he doesn't want to do, especially when he gets angry about it."

"It's hard. I just accepted the fact my mother needs me and there's no one else."

"I don't want it this way."

"Too bad. It is. Your mom let you believe life would be perfect. She was special, but she didn't accept reality. Till the end she thought she was going to change Jake, after how many years? I tried to tell her she could only change herself."

A knot begins to form at the base of my throat— a pulsing hurt.

Sandra reaches over. "I'm sorry, I didn't mean—"

"No, we're just talking, don't apologize."

"But not to make you feel bad. Certainly not that…when I moved back to the house to take care of Mama, I thought about all the fun you and I had here. But I had a lot of reality to face when Mama started forgetting what her fork was for, or when she tried to use her keys to open the green beans can. Then when we went to the doctor and got the diagnosis, it was like the rug was pulled out from under me. Maybe that's when reality really hit home, when I realized all my wishes weren't going to come true and I needed to face the fact I was living in a real world with real problems."

My mother always told me I was a princess, and my dreams were just around the corner, all I needed to do was have hope. I sigh, shake my head a little.

"I don't want to give up on hoping."

"I finally realized hope is accepting what is and knowing things are meant to be," Sandra says.

"Mom told me Prince Charming was on his way."

"Yeah, but she forgot to tell you he got lost at the Kmart."

"You think?"

"Tine? There are no Prince Charmings, thank God."

I look up, smile.

"Everything's going to be okay, Tine."

"I hope so."

Jake stood at the edge of the cliff by the lighthouse and looked down at the ocean. The night air was moist, but not cold. He hadn't been sure how to convince Christine she should go home without hurting her feelings. But he'd never wanted to be a burden to his kid, and now it looked like he was heading that way.

Maybe if he went along with everything she wanted, Christine would believe he was okay. Then she'd leave, get on with her life. He'd even let her and her friends help him with the lighthouse. That would make her feel better, convince her she could go back to Tucson.

Jake walked to the front of the lighthouse and studied the area where he'd seen Dorothy. He wanted her to come back so much he felt sick to his stomach. That's the only reason he'd come to the park tonight. The last few times he'd seen his wife, it had been here. When it happened, he felt good, as if his life was going to be okay.

Jake closed his eyes then slowly opened them. Where was she? He walked to the lighthouse, pushed the door open, then propped a brick against it. When he was in the middle of the lighthouse, he looked up at the night sky through the glass dome.

Where was she?

He clicked on the flashlight, glanced around. He'd accomplished a lot. The main room was clean, waiting for the electrical work to be installed and damaged walls to be replaced. Still feeling frustrated, he walked outside, clicked off the flashlight, sat on the bench and took a deep breath. Being surrounded by darkness felt good, peaceful. His hand throbbed. He'd thought taking on the lighthouse renovation would make him feel better, not so grief-stricken, but it wasn't working. Each day, he missed her more, thought about her more, and his heart kept breaking over and over.

Thank God, he hadn't told Christine about seeing Dorothy this morning. Smelling Dorothy's perfume had caught him off guard, almost kicked the words out of him.

Even though he hadn't said much in the kitchen, his daughter had stared at him with worry. Jake closed his eyes, wished when he opened them Dorothy would appear. But deep down, he knew she wouldn't come. And he missed her so much, he wasn't sure how much longer he could go on.

"Dust to dust," he whispered into the night air.

CHAPTER 13

I'm standing by the lighthouse, drenched in late afternoon sun. I'm here hoping to find my father so I can ask him to come home later and eat the dinner I managed to make. This morning, I went through my mother's cookbook and read all the notes she'd written next to different recipes. She'd marked which recipes we liked, which ones we hated. Beside one for meat loaf, she indicated that she'd thought I liked it a lot, but it was really Dad's favorite.

"Hey," Chet says, interrupting my thoughts.

"Hi, Chet. How are you?"

"Can't complain, no one wants to listen, anyway."

I laugh, shake my head. "That's true. I'm looking for my father. Do you know where he is?"

"Said he was going to Rent-All in Torrance. He'll

be back later. I came by this morning to see how things are going. Your dad's been working really hard. Thought I might help him some more."

"He's doing way too much." I have tried not to worry, but I just can't seem to stop myself.

"Yeah, he is, but he's a lot happier than he was."

"He works until it's dark, then he goes to the library or walks."

Chet nods, looks straight at me. "It's good you're here. Your father seems better since you came."

"Really?"

"Yeah, I think he was depressed before Christmas. I was worried about him, but then I found out you were coming home. Yesterday, at City Hall, he was telling people you were here for the holiday and decided to stay longer. Seemed proud of that."

I nod, don't know why. This doesn't sound like my father at all. But do I really know what he's like?

I didn't wait for Dad at the lighthouse. I came home, put on a heavier sweater because I opened the kitchen door and window in an effort to get the perfume out of the room, and now the house is freezing. Nobody seems to notice the perfume smell except me. I swear, every time I walk into this room, my mother's scent surrounds me.

More brisk air marches in, reminds me of when I was a kid, and I'd sit on the back porch step, wait for my father to come home so we could eat dinner. My mother would always come up behind me when she wanted me to come in, lift my hair, touch my cold skin with her warm hand. A moment later, she'd whisper, *"He'll be home soon."*

I turn toward the door to the dining room and wish she would push it open, walk into the kitchen, dark hair swaying, and her arms open.

Adam is standing on our front porch. Late morning sun surrounds him. I smile, wave through the picture window, and he smiles back. When I open the front door, he comes right in.

"Hi," I say, and we sit on the couch, at opposite ends.

"How are you?" he asks.

I smile again. He's such a nice guy. "Fine. I decided to stay until New Year's Day, like I planned. By then, my dad's hand will be a little better."

"Great. I stopped by the lighthouse to see him early this morning."

"And?"

"I took him some electrical supplies. He seemed happy about that. I told him I'd help him tomorrow. Plus, I checked the place out. I don't think it's going to be that big of a job. Shouldn't take more than three days to get the electricity in and the beacon turned on, with both of us working on it."

Relief fills my body, and for one quick moment, I want to scoot across the couch and hug Adam for just being here, helping my father.

"I'm so happy you're involved," I say instead.

"It'll be interesting."

"Thanks." I reach across, pat his shoulder.

"Your father and I talked for a while."

"He wasn't too busy working?"

"We worked, too. I helped him with the drywall. I told him you wanted to be closer to him and that you felt bad that you don't know each other that well."

"*What?*" I widen my eyes and imagine my father's face when Adam explained this to him.

"I told him you—"

"No, I heard you. Did Dad look at you like you're crazy or tell you to mind your own business?"

"He said you'd explained that, too. I thought that was enough. Means he was listening."

"But...he didn't tell you...?" I stop, can't quite decide what I want to ask.

"Your dad's like my uncle."

"The one who ran away with the lap dancer?"

"Let's hope not." Adam chuckles. "No, the one who lives in Hermosa Beach. He's a guy's guy. Not a lot of small talk going on, but my uncle's a decent man." Adam leans forward. "And Jake is, too."

I laugh. "Yeah, he is."

"Want my advice?"

"Do I have a choice?"

"Sure."

I nod. "Okay."

"Just go down to the lighthouse and help him. Don't ask if you can help, just do it. And don't try to change him or stop him, or give him any lip, just be with him. You can also keep an eye on his hand so he doesn't hurt it anymore."

"What if he won't let me help?" I think back to when I was a kid, and my chest begins to ache.

"Then accept that and forget it. I think he might surprise you."

I nod, don't think this will work, but I don't want to hurt Adam's feelings. "Okay, I'll try it. How else have you been?"

"Great. Sandra and I went out last night."

"You did?"

"Yeah, why do you sound so surprised?"

"I don't know. Did you have a good time?"

"We did. She's a good person. She told me about her mother. That's got to be tough."

"Yeah, it is. I've known Sandra for a long time, and you couldn't find a nicer person. God, doesn't this feel like high school?" I ask, leaning back.

Adam leans back, then smiles. "Yeah, isn't it great?"

And I have to admit it is.

My father rented a huge klieg light at Rent-All and he's put it inside the lighthouse so he can work after dark. The light is hooked to a generator that's running outside.

I go inside and find him pulling plastic red wires through a hole in the wall. In the harsh ar-

tificial rented light, his gray hair looks white—
unnatural.

"Dad," I say.

He turns a little, smiles. "Hi, honey."

There are huge circles under his eyes, and I realize he looks as if he's lost ten pounds. My heart hurts for him. "What are you doing?"

"Trying to get these wires where they need to be."

"Thought Adam was going to do all that?"

"Yeah, he is, but I want to do as much work as I can since he won't let me pay him." He pulls more wires out of the wall and begins untangling them.

"That's a very big light," I say, pointing to the massive drum in the corner.

"Isn't it great? I can work later."

"Do you want to come home and have some dinner? I made meat loaf, baked potatoes."

"You're becoming quite the cook."

"Mom once told me anyone can cook if they can read. So I just picked up her cookbook and started reading. Some of it's been pretty good. And she made notes by a lot of the recipes, the ones we liked. It's kind of like she's helping me." I swallow over the lump forming in my throat.

"Your mother was good that way," he says almost matter-of-factly, not looking at me.

"It would be nice if you'd take a break and come home for dinner."

He shakes his head, concentrates on the wires. "I'm doing this now. I'll be home later."

"Have you eaten?"

"Yeah, a hamburger from the café'." He gestures to a full sack in the corner by a Coke can. "I walked over there a little while ago."

"I can stay and help," I say, remembering what Adam said. I hug myself, glad that I put on a jacket. The ocean air feels wet and cold tonight.

"Not much you can do." He jerks the wires and a little part of the wall crumbles. "Damn," he says, then sighs.

I get the broom from the corner, begin sweeping up the debris.

"I'm getting a little too old for this," he says.

"You're not old. People live into their eighties, even nineties. There's no reason why you shouldn't, too."

Dad puts the wires down, sits on stacked drywall. "And some people don't live that long, either.

They get sick, things happen. You should know that."

I sit beside him. "But some do."

He rubs his face. His hands are filthy, and I see the black stitches sticking out covered in dust.

"How's your hand? Shouldn't you have it covered?"

"Probably, but it's hard to work with gloves on."

"When do you go to get the stitches out?"

"Probably won't. I can take them out myself."

"You should have the doctor do it, check it."

"Maybe I will, when I have time. Old guy like me, I can take out a few stitches." He looks at his stitches, shakes his head. "You should go home. It's pretty cold in here."

I think about leaving him, sitting in the warm kitchen, listening to music or watching TV. "I'll stay for a few minutes."

"You'll be ready to go back to Tuscon with all this work."

"Yeah, but it's lonely…."

"I understand lonely. You've got to think about your work."

"I've thought about that. It's a lot to give up, but

if I go back to Tuscon, I'll miss the ocean, the town, you." I say the last word without thinking. I'm not sure it's true. I miss my mother, and her death has left such a hole in my life—my heart, I wonder if I'm trying to fill it up with things and people close by.

"You're welcome to stay," he says. His voice is tired, his expression lifeless. "But I think you're making a mistake. You don't have to worry about me."

"What if I decided to live here for good?" The question pops out, surprising me, and I realize deep down I've been thinking about staying.

"Real estate around here is overpriced."

"I have enough to buy a small house."

"No reason to, I have plenty of room. But how could you leave what you've worked for?"

"I feel closer to Mom when I'm here, and I like that. You know, reading her cookbooks, going to places she loved."

"This place has a way of doing that." Dad rubs his face with his left hand, takes a deep breath. "I understand that."

I look around the lighthouse.

"You like what I've done?" he asks.

"I didn't think you'd get so much accomplished. I'm proud of you," I say. My mind is still on trying to decide if I really should move back. Is this what I want, need in my life, or am I trying to go back to a time that doesn't exist anymore?

"You know, you do that just like your mother."

"What?" I look at him, smile, happy that he's noticed something about me.

He nods toward my hands. "She used to cross her fingers when she was worried about something or trying to make a decision."

I look down, see that my right middle and index fingers are crossed. I laugh, uncross them. "I didn't even realize I was doing it."

He laughs. "She never did, either. I'd take her hand, uncross her fingers and then tell her not to worry."

One afternoon, she taught me to cross my fingers and make a wish—that my father would come home soon so we could eat dinner. I sat so close to my mother on the back porch that I could feel her warmth through my jeans. And her eyes looked as blue as my favorite crayon. I guess that's why it was my favorite.

"Christine," Dad says, bringing me back with such force, I blink.

"I'm sorry, what?"

"So do you really want to move back here? Is that what you want to do?"

"Have you ever wished for anything, Dad?"

"Wished? Not much."

"Mom and I used to cross our fingers and make wishes. She told me that I could make anything happen by just wishing, but I had to cross my fingers first." I feel light-headed, sad, yet I'm trying to conceal it.

"Your mother never lost hope with a lot of things."

"I'm not sure it was such a good idea to raise me to believe anything's possible. I'm forty-two, and I still think if I wish hard enough, things will change."

"I tried to tell her that. She didn't want you to get hurt. I think she raised you the way she thought I should have been raised. Things were different when we were kids."

"And how was that? You never talk much about when you were a kid."

He stares at me. I hold my hand up, cross my fingers, smile.

"I didn't know my father, and like I said, my mother was…let's just say she was a piece of work."

"Because of her drinking?"

"Yeah, when she drank she got mean. I took it when I was young, then I left at sixteen. I was afraid I was going to kill her, so I never saw her again."

"You're kidding?" Yet I can tell from his expression he's not.

"No, I'm not kidding."

"I'm sorry." I think about him, hating his mother so much. I can't imagine my life without loving mine the way I do, her joy of life, the way she loved me.

"No need to be. I did okay. Tried to do okay by you and your mother, too. I just never wanted to be any trouble to anyone. I learned that early."

"But that's what family is for, to help one another."

"I don't want anyone to have to worry about me," he insists.

"But isn't that what daughters are supposed to do?" I say, but don't know if this is true, and I wonder if I'll ever know.

Sandra and I have come to Cabrillo Beach. We are the only ones here, sitting on an old green army blanket that we found in her garage. Our bare feet are dug into the warm sand, our shoes sitting beside us.

Early afternoon sun warms my skin. The beach, a large sandy indentation against the earth, is almost as I remember it.

"Every place I go here, I'm surprised by the way things look. The park, here, they're smaller than I remember."

"Maybe it means you just don't see things like a kid anymore." She looks over, smiles. "I think we really grow up in our forties."

"How come you never left?" I ask, rubbing my hand against the sand.

"Because I like it here. I've never had a desire to move."

"I barely remember, but didn't our mothers bring us here every weekend one summer?"

Sandra nods. "Yeah. We'd walk down early, before daylight, watch the sun come up, then they'd cook breakfast, and we'd stay till midaf-ternoon." She gestures to the picnic tables, the small fire pits, and I can almost smell the wood burning.

"Didn't you ever want to try something new?" I ask.

Sandra leans back on her elbows, turns her face to the sun. "'New' isn't for me. I like knowing what's around every corner, at least where I live, anyway."

"I left because I wanted to experience life, see different places." A memory of me leaving for Phoenix flashes in my mind, my mother standing by my car, trying not to cry, telling me I was going to find a wonderful excitement that some people only dreamed about.

"You know, I never liked Phoenix. Then Albuquerque was too busy, dusty, and that's when I landed in Tucson," I say.

"Do you dislike Tucson enough to leave?" Sandra asks, holding her hands as if she is praying. "Please say yes."

"I told my father I might move back. What do you think?"

She turns a little. "You're ready to come home?"

"Maybe." I dig deep into the sand, grab a handful and sift it through my fingers.

Sandra looks over, grins. "You've had your adventure, and now it's time to come home. What did your dad say?"

"He said it was okay, that I could stay at the house. He's worried about my work, thinks I'm making a mistake by leaving my real estate business. In other words, he didn't seem overjoyed."

"Like men know how to show their feelings?"

"He also said he's worried he's going to be trouble for me."

"Trouble? You mean a burden?"

"Yeah, but he said trouble." I look down the beach, watch three seagulls pull at a plastic bag left by some irresponsible person. I dig deeper into the sand, find a shell and pull it out. It's one of those tiny ice-cream cone shells, a spiral of white and beige—like fine china.

One time my mother brought me here, and we were picking up beach stones, and I told her I wanted to look for shells instead. She took my hand, smiled.

You'll find what you need, Chrissy, just be patient.

A little while later I found a smooth beach stone that had a fossil imprint of an ice-cream cone shell on it. I was so happy.

I laugh.

"What?"

"My mother told me once, maybe more than once, that I'd find what I need if I was patient. You think I ever will?"

"Don't know. Adam would say you already have it."

"I don't get some of what he says."

"Guess that's okay, too." Sandra leans back again. "I love it here when no one else is around. I couldn't imagine not living in San Pedro." She looks out to the ocean and we watch a wave crash on the shore.

"What I want to know is how do I go from daughter to someone who might have to take care of my father?"

"When Mama started showing signs..." Sandra's voice catches. I look over at her, pat her hand.

"You'll do it. Your father is healthy, so enjoy

that, take advantage of it. When Mama got sick, I'd try to tell her something or help her, and she didn't want to hear it. We'd argue. She was getting more and more paranoid because of her memory loss. It was one of the toughest things I've ever done. Your mother helped a lot."

I picture my mother crossing the two yards, going into Josephine's kitchen. What was she thinking?

"She's not getting better," Sandra says.

I look over at her, shake my head, feel my heart hurt.

"Adam drove me to the nursing home last night and I talked to Loellen. Mama's not eating, she walks the halls day and night, unless she's medicated like a zombie. Her weight's down to nothing. I have this feeling she's going to wear out."

I press my lips together, pat her hand. What can I say that won't sound trite? There's nothing.

"Adam made me feel a little better," Sandra says, with a half smile.

"How much better?"

"Not second base better." She laughs, and so do I. "But that may happen someday. I finally realized he's fun. He took me to see Mama, sat in the hallway for thirty minutes so she wouldn't be afraid, and then he came in later. He was so kind to her, talked to her as if she were really listening. I sat there and thought he's weird, not perfect, but what guy would do this?"

"Not many."

"Then we went to the Crab Catcher, had dinner. He's so upbeat. I need that right now."

I nod, swallow back tears. I close my eyes, realizing that nothing in my life is the same.

CHAPTER 14

When I got home from the beach, I shook the sand out of my tennis shoes and left them on the back porch. Now I'm walking around the kitchen in bare feet. The room *still* smells like my mother's perfume.

Dad actually did dishes. The kitchen looks perfect, the way it used to be all the time. I walk back to my room to get sandals. My black suitcase, standing by the closet, looks as if it's waiting for me to pack it.

A dull feeling moves through me, telling me I don't want to go back to Tucson. But is this the right thing to do? I've made so many mistakes in my life, yet I've accomplished a lot, too.

I walk back to the kitchen. If I move, I'll have to hire a moving company, see if my colleague, Kathy, would send me my personal things and ship my car. And it would be such a big change.

I get out the phone book, open it to real estate agencies. There are plenty in San Pedro—Century 21, Prudential, the one I work for now. I could easily transfer my work here, be where my mother's perfume lingers. I write down the office number, just in case I make up my mind.

I'm standing on the porch, enjoying the sunset. Adam and Sandra pull out of her driveway in his red truck. Sandra waves, says something to Adam, and he stops the truck in front our house. I walk to the passenger side and lean in through the open window.

"Hi, you two." For a brief moment, I feel like I'm thirteen, watching Sandra leave on a date. I always wanted to go with her, be almost grown-up, mysterious, sitting next to a boy, smiling like she is now.

"I had fun at the beach today," I say, and she nods.

"I did, too."

"Where are you going?" I ask, feeling the breeze against my face.

"To see Mama." Sandra looks over at Adam and her worried expression softens just a tiny bit.

Adam grins at me. "I helped your father this morning. The electrical work is coming along. He knows more than I thought. He might make his deadline."

"That's good."

"A welder buddy of mine said he'll help secure the stairs. I think the place will be safe in a week. The beacon could be on soon, if we get lucky and get all the parts."

"My father's going to let someone help him with the stairs?"

"Does he have a choice? We were laughing today, had a pretty good time. He knows he can't do them himself. He gets focused on something and doesn't say much, but he didn't seem to mind me being down there or mentioning the lighthouse to my friend."

"Is there anything I can help with?"

"Lots of trash to pick up. The fence needs to be worked on. Now, that's a girl job." He laughs and Sandra swats his arm.

"She doesn't need a *girl's* job. Hey, you want to come with us?" She scoots over, pats the space beside her. Before I can say no, she reaches over and opens the passenger-side door.

I step aside, then lean in against the seat. "I'd better stay home."

"Why?"

"Well, I…don't want to be the third wheel."

"Come on. We need the company. Your dad won't be home. We'll get you back early. We're going to see Mama and then get something to eat."

The house is clean. I made dinner for my father, if he ever comes home. And most of all, I'm tired of being alone.

I climb in, close the door, and there is a tiny kernel of the same feeling I had when I was young and Sandra would let me ride around with her and whoever she was dating.

"This is like old times," I say.

"Sure is."

Adam slips the truck into gear, looks over at us. "What's that all about?"

"Nothing," I say, not wanting to mention Sandra's boyfriends from high school.

She laughs. "You can tell him. Oh, I'll tell him. When we were young, I used to let her ride around with me and my boyfriends. She was a real pain, but I put up with her cause she looked so lonely. Still does."

"So now I'm your boyfriend?"

"No."

Sandra and Adam laugh together, as though they really like each other—such a difference from the other night at the bar.

When we get to the nursing home, I am happy Sandra isn't alone. The parking lot is almost empty and depressing in the dusky light. We walk three abreast, until we come to the front door. The security guard lets us in, and we go down the slick, quiet hallway to Josephine's room.

"You guys better wait out here for a little while," Sandra says. "I might have to calm her down. It's hard for Mama when there are a lot of people around."

"Don't rush," Adam says, touches her shoulder.

She smiles a grateful smile, and Adam watches until she disappears into the room.

He and I lean against the white wall. I sigh. "How does my father look, sound to you?" I whisper, trying not to disturb Sandra.

"Okay. He looks tired, but he's been busting his hump. He's doing what he wants and that's important."

"I guess. I just can't get past the fact he might hurt himself."

"And if he does, what's the worst that could happen?"

I look at Adam, think about my father in the hospital with a concussion or broken back. "He could break his back, a leg, be stranded there."

Adam turns, faces me. His expression is so serious. "Come on, let's take a walk."

We move slowly past white room after white room. Some doors are ajar, some wide open. I look in every once in a while, see a lump in a bed, then drop my gaze.

"You know your problem?" Adam finally says quietly.

"Don't you mean problems?"

"Only one that I can see. You don't trust in what's been set up for you."

"*Set up* for me? Is this some Zen thing?"

"Kind of. You try to manipulate life and not let it happen, let it unfold naturally. Think about it. At least you have your dad, and not what Sandra is dealing with." He gestures back to Josephine's room. "Now, there's a problem."

"But my father used to be so conservative."

"So he's changing. He lost his wife, and he's getting older. You aren't the same since we drove here. We change every minute, every second. You keep wasting time and energy worrying about what is out of your hands. You are probably talking to your dad more than you ever have. If he was the same, you wouldn't have made that kind of progress."

"I'm just not used to worrying about him, that's all. It's hard."

"Life isn't easy or fair. Never will be. You think any of these people think that? Anticipated this? You need to let yourself believe that things are going to work out, one way or another. We can't force life to be what we want."

"You certainly are serious tonight." I look at him and he lifts a brow, nods, but says nothing. "I'll think about all this."

We pass more doors, more lumps, a few muffled TVs. When we get back to Josephine's room, Sandra is waiting for us in the hall. Her face is red, swollen from crying, but she smiles—and I feel guilty as hell for complaining.

"Do you want to go in?" she asks.

How could I say no?

I walk in first. The room is dark, except for a small

light on the table. Josephine is in bed, covered, and her legs are pulled up—a lump. My heart hurts for her. The three of us stand around her hospital bed, Sandra and Adam on one side, me on the other.

Adam lightly touches Josephine's forearm. Her skin is so white. "Hey, Josephine, how are you?"

She doesn't answer, doesn't turn. Her eyes are open, yet she doesn't blink.

"I brushed her hair." Sandra strokes the red strands gently against the pillow and the tips of my fingers tingle.

"Josephine, you have beautiful hair, just like Sandra." Adam brings his arm around Sandra's shoulders. "You also have a lovely daughter. She's wonderful."

There is no movement, nothing, and I wonder how much a human heart can stand.

It's 10:00 a.m., and I'm outside the lighthouse. I slept late, woke up feeling good. Seeing Josephine, knowing what Sandra has to go through, took a lot out of me yesterday, but this morning I thought about what Adam said. Maybe he's right; anyway, I'm willing to try. I'm going to help my father, or try anyway.

I look up. The sun is suspended in a perfect sky. There are no clouds, just beautiful blue extending forever. It is the kind of sky my mother would love. She'd wrap her arms around me and tell me today was made just for me.

I walk into the circular room, breathe the dark, cool air. The large klieg light that Dad rented sets quietly in the corner. Brilliant sunlight cascades from the glass dome, erasing shadows and making a sunlit ring in the middle of the room.

Dad is working on the far wall, painting new drywall.

"Adam, I've got wiring I need you to check," he says.

"It's only me."

He turns around, smiles. "Sorry. I thought you were Adam. He said he'd come by." He puts the paint roller down, crosses his arms and puffs out his cheeks for a moment.

"Tired?"

"Yeah, I'm beat. I've been at this since five." He digs a small slip of paper out of his pocket, squints at it. "I forgot to call Chet. He's gonna come down and help me carry the extra drywall out of here."

"Maybe I can help you." I cross the area between us, stand in the middle, in the circle of sunlight.

"Drywall's too heavy for you."

I make a muscle with my right arm. "I'm pretty strong."

He laughs. "You don't look strong."

"I work out. Lift weights."

"You do?"

"Yeah, I joined a gym last year. I told Mom." I suddenly realize how much he doesn't know about me. "Didn't she tell you? I won a membership because I was top salesperson for the quarter. So I decided to use it."

"Maybe I forgot."

"You know, Mom was our buffer."

"Buffer?"

"Like in *The Godfather, Part II*. Some guys were buffers, the middlemen."

He laughs, rubs his chin. "I guess so."

"I went to see Josephine last night, with Sandra and Adam." I walk back to the edge of the room, sit on the floor and press my back against the wall. An image of Josephine in bed—so silent—sneaks into my mind. I shake my head in an effort to make it go away, but it won't budge.

Dad folds the paper, puts it back in his pocket. He comes over, stands in front of me.

"How is she?"

His words rush at me, like the ocean, knocking me down a little.

I swallow, think about my mother crossing the backyards to Josephine's. She probably had so much hope that her friend would get better. In a way, I'm glad she didn't live to see the way Josephine is today.

"Christine."

I look up. "I think she's dying, Dad," I manage to say.

He sits beside me.

Foggy images of my mother's memorial service float through my mind: my father and I, standing next to each other on the hill at Green Hills Cemetery; the ocean breeze touching my skin; the town where I grew up, far below. I have not thought of this day in months.

"She's dying?" Dad asks, squinting.

"The medicine doesn't work sometimes, so she

doesn't rest. When it does, she just lies there, doesn't speak, doesn't move."

"I didn't know she was that bad."

"What is Sandra going to do?" I turn, look at him, study his face and want to hear an answer my mother would give me.

"Sandra will be okay, honey."

He's so pale. "You look really tired, Dad. Are you sleeping?"

"I'm hanging in there. Sandra's a strong kid."

"But if something happens, she won't have anyone. I hate to think of her all alone. Josephine is in bad shape, but at least she's still here."

"She'll be okay."

"It's sad. Remember how Josephine and Mom used to pal around? They were always over at each other's house, talking, laughing, taking us places when we were kids. Last night, Josephine didn't even move."

"I didn't see much of your mother and Josephine together. I guess your mother did those things when I was on a trip." He moves closer, faces me. "Maybe you shouldn't go to the nursing home if it upsets you."

"I went for Sandra. The parking lot is always deserted. She checks on her at night."

Dad studies the concrete floor, shakes his head.

"But it's going to be awful, when she dies," I say.

"Maybe not so awful."

"What do you mean?" I stand, cross my arms, too.

"What kind of life does Jo have? Her husband is gone, and look what this situation is doing to her daughter," he says.

"But she's still alive, maybe that's a comfort to Sandra."

"Not many parents want to be a burden to their kids."

I step forward, want to hug him, be hugged, but he pulls the piece of paper out of his pocket, reads it as if it's the most important thing in the world.

"I'd better call Chet," he says, then turns and walks across the room.

CHAPTER 15

Jake clutched the cold metal railing and looked down at the waves. The ocean sounds soothed him. Tonight, more than other nights, he needed to feel connected to something.

He clicked on the flashlight, shined the light against the night sky, then clicked it off and put it in his back pocket. Just when he didn't think he could stand being alone any longer, Dorothy always appeared. And tonight, more than ever, he wanted to feel hopeful again.

Jake grabbed the railing then let go, straightened, and sucked in a deep breath. He was exhausted. He'd worked too many hours on the lighthouse today, trying to finish in time.

Jake closed his eyes and opened them quickly. All he wanted was to see Dorothy one more time. He would be satisfied with that and then he could go on.

"No," Jake whispered, and crossed his arms. He'd never be satisfied without Dorothy. He leaned over the railing again. Why wasn't he recovering from her death? Other guys lost their wives, got over the grief, the tragedy. Why couldn't he?

His stomach tingled, the way it had when he was twenty-three, learning to fly, and worried whether he was going to live through the training, through all his mistakes. At the height of his troubles, he'd met Dorothy. As they got to know each other, he'd thought he was superior to her. He didn't give a damn about anyone, and she'd cared so much. He'd only wanted female companionship for one thing— getting laid. Back then, life was about taking chances, pushing the enve-lope as far as he could before he fell off the edge.

He'd prided himself on being cold, distant, and not giving a crap about life. Yet, he found he couldn't hide his feelings from Dorothy. She tasted life from the inside out and could almost read his mind. She accepted him the way he was, battered, damaged goods, and loved him no matter what he said or did. She did this, even when she found he didn't want their child. From the beginning, he'd told her he never wanted kids, knew he wasn't the father type. What he hadn't told her was that he sensed some genetic connection with his mother's abuse—he didn't want to be anything like her. That was one of the reasons he quit drinking after Christine was born. He wasn't going to take any chances.

But one day, Dorothy had come to him, looking so serious. She'd held his hand and told him the world was going to be okay with another human being in it. *They'd* be okay. He'd argued with her all night, tried to convince her to have an abortion, but she refused. He'd never told her the entire story about his mother, how abusive she was. He was too ashamed. He and Dorothy fought bitterly, and she cried so hard, he thought she was going to choke. He didn't understand her then, never really understood her, until now.

Now he knew Dorothy loved everybody and everything in this world and wanted love back.

That night, he finally gave up and told her the baby was going to be her responsibility and not to expect any help from him. In the morning, she explained she'd do it all, he'd see. He could remain on the sidelines and watch, wouldn't have to get involved.

Then she grabbed his hand, held it tightly and told him to *believe*. Neither of them ever anticipated that someday she might not be around.

How could he *believe* now?

"Believe," he whispered. The ocean breeze touched his face, his injured hand.

A few times, when she was pregnant, Dorothy and he had held each other in the evenings. She opened all the windows, and the ocean air came in, as if it was searching for them. Dorothy turned off the lights and they lay on the rug, shadows painting their skin, quiet covering them like a blanket. One time, his hand rested on her belly and he felt the baby move, and Dorothy sighed ever so lightly.

What had she wanted him to *believe* in?

Hadn't the miracle of their life together been enough?

It's New Year's Eve. Adam and I are sitting in the kitchen. The window over the sink is open and the breeze has made the room cool. I broiled steaks a little while ago, and the place got really smoky.

This afternoon, I went to the store, bought T-bones, potatoes, romaine lettuce, tomatoes and mushrooms, then called Sandra and told her I was cooking whether she liked it or not. I also asked my father to join us, but he said he was busy, and he'd eat a sandwich at the lighthouse. I'm a little more used to his reactions now, but I still worry he's not eating enough, that he's working way too hard, and this afternoon I tried to say something, but he wouldn't listen to me.

The evening breeze, sharp with the cool taste of the ocean, weaves around us, lifts a corner of my napkin, floats it above the spotted Formica table for a moment, then it rests against the table.

"Too bad your father couldn't have dinner with us," Adam says. He gets up, picks up our plates and takes them to the sink. Sandra is in the living room, calling the nursing home to check on her mother.

"I asked him twice, but he *wouldn't* come, not couldn't. He's down at the lighthouse working his brains out."

Adam nods, doesn't give me a Zenism or an Adamism. I get up, begin rinsing dishes in steamy water, then loading them in the dishwasher.

Sandra walks into the kitchen. Her face is white, her lips pulled into a thin line.

"You okay?" I ask, then dry my hands and go to her. I drape an arm around her shoulders and give her a hug.

"Yeah, I'm fine." She walks over to the sink and just stands there. "Just leave the dishes, I'll do them."

"I like doing dishes," Adam says.

She looks at him, laughs a little. "Oh, you do not. Nobody likes doing dishes." She glances at me. "Then again, maybe he does."

"I do. When the dishes are finished, it looks like I've accomplished something. One moment the kitchen's a wreck, the next—" his fingers open close fast "—kapow, fantastic." He walks to the sink, Sandra steps aside, and Adam begins rinsing forks and knives.

"How's your mother?" I ask.

"The same." She shakes her head, looks directly

at me. "No, I need to face this. She's worse. The nurse says the dosage of medicine they're giving her isn't working. She's getting more and more agitated, so the doctor is going to up the dosage. Now she'll be more of a zombie than ever. Plus it's hard on her heart, her lungs."

Adam and I look at each other and I press my lips together. What can I say?

We clean the table, rinse the broiler pan and salad bowls in silence. When we're finished Sandra groans, sits at the table, and we join her.

"Want to go see her?" Adam asks, taking her hand and holding it gently.

"Yes, but I'm so tired of that nursing home. What a way to spend New Year's Eve. I just want to scream. How much longer can I go there?"

Adam rubs her fingers, and his gaze grows so concerned.

"We all can ride up there. I don't mind," I say, trying to be a good friend. But I hate the place already with its lumpy rooms, the smell, the sadness. I can imagine how Sandra feels.

She looks at me, smiles a little. "Going with people does make it easier. I didn't realize how lonely I was until you guys started coming with me. I just thought I was doing okay."

"You are doing okay, honey," I say. "You're doing better than anyone could. We can go there anytime you want. Right, Adam?"

He smiles, squeezes her hand, and I love him for it. "Of course."

"What about your father? He has to be hungry. Maybe we should take him some food on the way." Sandra gestures toward the stove.

"Yeah, let's go by the lighthouse with a plate, and then over to the nursing home," Adam says. "It'll be good for Jake to eat a real meal."

We get up, and I look at both of them, realize I don't have this circle of friendship and support in Tucson. Maybe, coming home, I've found a part of me I didn't even know was missing.

It's 8:00 a.m.

"I came to help you," I say, standing in the middle of the circle of sun that's shining through the glass dome of the lighthouse.

Dad looks over. He was gone when I got up this morning so I don't know how long he's been here.

"You don't have to help me," he says. "I thought you were going home today."

"I canceled my reservation last night, and I want to help you. Adam said the fence has to be fixed. I could work on that."

"Yeah, some boards need to be hammered back into place. I checked it yesterday. Some need to be replaced. But you aren't going home?"

"I guess I need some nails and a hammer, right?" I look around the round room.

Dad chuckles. "Yeah, those would help get the job done. I also bought new pickets for the empty spaces."

"And where would I find all this stuff?"

He walks over to me. "You don't have to help. I'll get to the fence eventually."

"It'll give me something to do. The house is clean, we have five days' worth of leftovers in the refrigerator, so I'm cooked out."

Dad shakes his head. "Well, when you put it that way, you might as well work."

I am standing looking at the fence. My father and I worked on it for three hours. It's almost finished and I have to say, it looks good, straight, sturdy—like a child dressed for her first day of school. I told Dad tomorrow I'll paint it.

I just came back from the house. I went home to get a couple of Cokes out of the fridge for us, and I'm still holding the cold bottles, one in each hand. I walk through the gate and into the lighthouse. Dad looks over and I smile, hold up the Cokes, cross to where he is.

"Here you go," I say. We open the bottles at the same time and they hiss. I sit on the concrete floor, my back against the new drywall, and Dad joins me.

"Thanks for helping," he says, and takes a sip of his Coke, licks his lips. "This is good, nice and cold."

"Working on the fence wasn't that hard. Kind of fun, actually. I think I did a good job." I worked slowly and it took me some time to learn how to nail the pickets into the boards. Dad showed me, and I finally caught on. Then he went back into the lighthouse and worked on the drywall, but every once in a while he came out to check on me.

"I don't know if I'd call it fun, but you did do a

good job," he says. "That's how I feel when I'm working here, like I'm really getting something done."

"Remember when I used to try to help you wash the car? I don't even know how old I was, but today kind of reminded me of that. Except this time, I actually got to do the work."

Dad doesn't look over, just nods. "Yeah, you used to want to squirt the hose and you'd get me all wet. Then you'd try to dry the hood and you couldn't reach places and you'd jump up and scratch the paint."

"You said I was too slow."

"I was in a big hurry when I was younger. Always had more things to do than I had time for."

"After you ran me off, I'd go into the kitchen, Mom would fan my neck because I was all sweaty, get me a Coke." I hold up my half-empty bottle. "She'd tell me she loved me, that you loved me."

Dad looks up to the lighthouse dome for a long moment and I see his eyes narrow, tiny wrinkles appear and fan back to his hairline.

"You know, Christine, sometimes people change too late. It's a lot of work being a good parent."

I close my eyes, and fatigue sweeps over my body. I remember lying in bed, hearing my mother whisper my father's name after he'd lost his temper with me—*Oh, Jake, she needs you to believe in her.*

Dad clears his throat, and I return to the moment.

"Dorothy always tried to make things right between you and me."

I don't say anything, swallow over the lump in my throat. With the lighthouse door open, I can hear the rhythm of the ocean far below.

"You did okay," I say, although I don't really mean it. But I like sitting here talking with him and I don't want to ruin it. I study him. He's still staring straight ahead. "Everybody makes mistakes. I've made plenty. I don't have to tell you that," I add.

He clears his throat again. "Damned plaster dust." He looks at me, nods. "You know, I never called in sick a day in thirty-two years with the airline. Your mother sometimes wanted me to for your birthday, Christmas, but I wouldn't."

"Why not?"

"My military training. Didn't want someone flying my mission. But I forgot how important your mother was to me, how she asked for so little. All she ever wanted was for me to be a father to you, to be happy like she was."

"Nobody's perfect," I say, not really meaning this, either. It's just something to fill up the silence. "I came out okay." I think about what Sandra told me, how my mother used to complain to her. I want to ask my father about this, but how can I?

"I should have done better," he says, rubbing his face. "But I just didn't know how."

Jake sat on the park bench and breathed deeply. A moment ago, he watched Christine walk across the stretch of grass toward home. Today she'd worked hard on the fence that Dorothy had loved so much. And he'd made a stab at explaining to her how he wished he'd been a better father, a better husband. He didn't know how to tell her he hadn't wanted her, and then, when she was born, how he hadn't trusted himself to be a father.

He stood, stretched his arms over his head and

groaned. The park was growing thick with shadows. A wave of grief rolled in, overtaking any happiness from the day, clouding his mind, and he sat on the bench again. He shut his eyes and demanded Dorothy come to him.

"Dorothy," he heard himself say. It was the first time he'd said her name in months. He stood, turned and held his head back, looked up at the dark sky and closed his eyes. Then he stared into the dark. He raised his arms with his fingers stretched wide, and he was sure he could feel the pulsing of the earth.

CHAPTER 16

"I am so sorry," I say, knowing my words are insufficient.

Sandra is standing in front of me, dabbing a soggy Kleenex to her eyes, crying. I'm sitting at her kitchen table, feeling as if I've been punched in the stomach. Ten minutes ago, she phoned to tell me Josephine passed away this morning. I threw on jeans, a T-shirt and ran across our backyards.

"I shouldn't have called so early. I didn't mean to wake you." Her voice ripples with tears.

I go to her, hug her hard, guide her to the booth in her kitchen, and she sits where I was sitting a moment ago. "Have you had anything to eat?"

She shakes her head. "I'm not hungry. Can you imagine me not hungry? How crazy is that?"

"How about some hot chocolate? I think we

both could use some." I go to the fridge, find what I need and then pull mugs out of the cabinet. I'm dodging in and out of feelings—sadness Josephine is gone, weariness over my own grief, a numb disbelief. I work at quieting the storm in my chest.

A few minutes later, I place a steaming mug in front of my friend. Sandra cups her hands around it, looks up and gives me a wan smile. "Thanks."

"Do you need to go over to the nursing home?" I ask, taking a seat across from her.

"There's no reason. The coroner picked up Mama's body this morning. She wanted to be cremated and then buried in the cemetery. I made all the arrangements months ago. My supervisor at the hospice made sure I did that. I just didn't think it would happen so soon."

"Maybe it's always too soon."

She takes a sip of her chocolate. "You know if it wasn't so early I'd put some bourbon in here."

"It's never too early, honey. You need it." I get up and find the bourbon bottle in a cabinet over the stove, pour a shot in hers and mine, and the hot chocolate edges the rims of the mugs.

"You think I should?" She looks up at me.

"Yeah, I think you should."

"I didn't believe this was going to happen. How stupid am I?" she says, her eyes wide, so red.

"Your mother's been sick for a long time. You said the other night you knew she was fading."

"Yeah, saying it and having it happen are two very different things."

"I know." It was 6:04 in the evening when my father called me, told me about my mother. I'd just looked at the clock, told myself I needed to think about dinner. A few times I had wondered what I would do if my father died. I knew I would come home, support and help my mother. I never dreamed she would be first. When Dad told me, my world turned wavy. I sat back on the couch, my head full, my throat tight, everything around me shimmery, floating.

Sandra sighs.

"Okay?"

"Yeah, I guess. Yesterday when I went to see Mama, I knew. You know, I just had one of those feelings she wasn't going to be here much longer. I brushed her hair for a long time, held her hand until the meds kicked in and she fell asleep."

"You had a feeling?"

"It's hard to explain, but I knew she was going to die. I told Adam. He said I should trust my feelings, but I kept shaking them off." Sandra brings the tissue to her eyes, rubs them, begins to cry again. I watch her, see myself in her actions. I swallow my tears, pat her hand, want to comfort her.

"Last night I called the nursing home three times before I went to bed. I finally went to sleep about ten. At three, I sat straight up, and my heart was beating so fast. Right before I had this feeling that she was hugging me. I thought I was dreaming, maybe I was, but it didn't feel like it. Five minutes later, the phone rang and they told me she'd just passed away five minutes before."

"Maybe it's a sign. Your mother loved you so much."

"Adam said—" A sob takes her words away. She wipes her eyes again. "I wish I had stayed, been there. Why did she have to be alone? She hated being alone."

I hold her hand tightly. "You didn't know. How could you know?" But the hairs on the back of my neck are standing up. "Maybe she wasn't alone, maybe Loellen was with her."

"I didn't want her to be by herself. You know what a good mother she was. I should have been there for her."

I think about my own regret, my mother in her car, on the highway by herself, and my stomach twists. I feel more numb.

"I complained about going to the nursing home, now I don't have to go anymore."

"Anyone would have complained, honey," I say. "You were a good daughter. Your mother knew that. You did your best."

Sandra looks at me and gives me a tearful smile. "Mama would have wanted you to be here with me. I'm so glad you didn't go back to Tucson yesterday. Maybe it was meant to be that you stayed."

Sandra, Adam and I are in Josephine's room. Adam came over to Sandra's house as soon as I called him, and then she and I followed him in his truck to the nursing home. Adam and I tried to talk her out of coming here so soon, but she insisted that she wanted to clean out her mother's room so she wouldn't have to come back later.

"What do you want to do with everything?" I ask. I'm by the stripped hospital bed, trying not to look at the plastic mattress cover. There isn't a lot in the room—just Josephine's red chair, clothes in the closet, a few books, personal items in the small bathroom.

"Mama loved that chair," Sandra says, then turns to the window, looks out past where I saw her mother's reflection days ago.

Adam puts his arm around Sandra, and she tries to smile.

"My uncle always said death is hardest on the ones left behind," he says.

We nod, look at each other.

"I almost forgot. Mama has a brother in New York."

I shake my head. "I didn't know that."

"They weren't close. He lives in the city. I guess I should call him later."

"Probably," Adam says.

"Her chair." Sandra nods toward it. "I'd like to take it home. But her clothes, what should I do with them?" She walks to the closet, fingers a white blouse, as if in a trance. "You know, I don't think I can do this."

"We can leave if you want," I say.

"No, I need to do this. I don't want strangers touching her things."

"The chair will fit in my truck," Adam says. "That's no problem. The clothes… Christine and I could take them to Goodwill."

"I can't let you do all that," she says.

When my mother died, I was so stunned, so heartbroken, I went back to Tucson two days after her memorial service. I needed to run, get away from all the memories. And now our house is still full of my mother's belongings—as if they're waiting for her.

"Don't worry, I'll take care of everything," I say.

"There's not much, she didn't need much." Sandra looks at me; her face shows her fatigue, and her eyes are so red and puffy.

I hug her. "Don't worry about any of this. Adam and I will take care of everything. You should go home, call your uncle, rest a little."

"Maybe I will."

* * *

I've come to the lighthouse to tell my father about Josephine. Adam and I drove Sandra home, then we went back and cleaned out Josephine's room. We got an orderly to help carry the chair to his truck, and while that was being done, I folded the few blouses, sweaters, pants and nightclothes and stacked them on the bed. Then a nurse brought in a box and asked me what I was going to do with the clothes. She talked about how much she liked Sandra and Josephine. All I could do was stare, nod once in a while, because I was thinking about how I would never see Josephine again.

I threw everything else away—her brush, tooth-brush, soap, underwear. I think Josephine would have liked that I did this—someone who cared. Then Adam and I drove to the Goodwill on Pacific and Tenth and dropped off the boxes of clothes.

"Dad," I say, walking into the lighthouse.

"Yeah?"

He's at the top of the spiral staircase, near the lighthouse beacon. Sun washes through the glass dome, turning his hair to silver, surrounding his body with light.

I blink. "Did you get the stairs fixed?"

He looks down over the railing. "Yeah, Adam's friend came and rewelded the entire staircase, made sure the risers are secure. He worked all day."

"The place looks good." I'm still surprised at how much work he's gotten done, how everything has come together, fitting perfectly, like a puzzle.

He walks down the spiral staircase, hands on both railings.

"What's wrong?" he asks when he gets to the bottom.

Maybe it's the tension or all the sadness that has been welling up in my heart, but I burst into tears, cover my face with my hands, feel so embarrassed.

"Christine?" Dad says softly. "Why are you crying?" His arm goes around my shoulder and he pats me. Then the warmth is gone. More tears flood from my eyes.

"Josephine died early this morning," I say between sobs. The storm in my chest swirls higher, wider. In the shimmery light, I see my father's face crumble, the circles under his eyes deepen.

"I feel so sorry for Sandra," I say. "It's hard to lose

your mother." Deep anguish pours out of me, and I cry harder, double over and moan.

"That's too bad. That's just a terrible shame. What happened?"

I shake my head, unable to talk because I'm crying so hard. I sit on the cold concrete, cry more.

"What happened?" my father asks again.

I sniff, wipe my eyes. "The doctor said her heart gave out. Sandra says it happens a lot with Alzheimer's patients. They just wear down." I hear Sandra's soft words, remember her grief-ravaged expression and begin crying again.

"What a shame." Dad sits on the third step, puts his head in his hands, rubs his face, then looks up. "I guess I didn't realize she was that bad. She was your mother's best friend."

"We cleaned out what little she had at the nursing home. Adam and I took her clothes to the Goodwill, brought her red chair home."

"Yeah," Dad says, nods.

"Dad?"

He looks at me.

"Why haven't you gotten rid of Mom's things?"

I hear the ocean rushing against the earth.

"Dad?"

"I tried, but I couldn't. Every time I started to pack them away, I thought about her in her car, all alone. I'd just walk out of the room. I guess I felt if her things were gone then she'd never come back. Stupid."

I cross the space between us. My face is hot, my eyes swollen and sore. I stand in front of him. "She's not coming back, Dad."

He nods.

"I could go through Mom's clothes and give them to charity, if you want me to. The Goodwill was grateful for Josephine's clothes, and Mom would like that her things would be helping people."

I expect him to say *no*, stand up and go back to *work*, but he doesn't.

"Maybe that would be best. I guess it's time. But I didn't want you to have to do it."

"I don't mind. I just didn't think about it till today."

He gets up, starts picking up extra wiring and paper, and I go over to him. "Let me help you."

Dad looks at me, tries to smile. "Your mother

used to say that same thing when I was working around the house. There are times you remind me so much of her."

"What would she say?"

"*Let me help you.* She always wanted to do her part, make us a family."

We begin picking up the debris, putting it in a large garbage bag.

"She always wanted to help. Sometimes I yelled because she didn't do things the way I wanted her to," he says.

"Like when I tried to wash the car."

He nods. "She had this idea we could do things together. That's why she wanted to buy our house."

"I always thought it was you who wanted the house."

"No, your mother loved the place the first time she saw it. It would have been more practical to buy a tract home in Torrance, but she wanted a house with some history, one that was by the lighthouse, the ocean."

"Are you glad you bought the house?"

He nods. "It made your mother happy. I didn't think we could pay for it. I was worried about losing my job, you know how airlines are, but I gave in. She kept telling me I should believe, have hope. Now I'm glad I bought it. She told me she loved the house because it had grown old gracefully, and she wanted to do that."

I cross the space and put chips of drywall in the garbage bag.

"This is nice," I say.

"What?"

"Talking, sharing memories."

He ties the bag, studies it. "Did your mother ever tell you when you were born she thought you looked like an ice-cream cone?"

I laugh, feel the fullness in my chest. "That's so like Mom. Why'd she think that?"

"Back then nurses wrapped all the babies really tight in blue or pink blankets. Dorothy said with your head sticking out and the blanket wrapped cone-shaped, you looked like a human ice-cream cone."

"Did you think so?"

"I'm not much of a baby person. Your mother took care of all that."

How many stories haven't we shared? I look

around, shadows are falling into the room. "We should turn on the light if we're going to stay and work."

"Right." Dad goes out and I hear the generator kick on. He comes back, hits the klieg switch, and light showers through the room.

"I feel so sad about Josephine," I say.

He looks at me, and his eyes narrow a little. "Sometimes you can't save people no matter what you do, honey. Remember that."

I shake my head, think about my mother's accident, wish life could be different. "Why did she have to be on the freeway?" I'm thinking out loud, really.

"I don't have an answer, but I wish it had been me. She was going to get some plants for the yard. I didn't want her to buy anything else. She went, anyway."

"Oh."

"You know she was the only person who believed in me."

My chest begins to throb, and I look at him.

"When I was flying in Nam, I'd get these feelings that your mother was close by, that she was thinking about me and that made me feel better."

As a little girl, I looked through old scrapbooks my mother made—Dad's fading photographs, his unlined face—someone I didn't know, a kid who grew up to be my father.

He stares at me. "Christine, don't ever forget there are some things in this world we can't change, can't prevent," he says softly, and then walks slowly out of the lighthouse.

CHAPTER 17

Jake stood in the middle of the lighthouse's main room. In the last few days, he'd worked harder than he'd ever worked in his life. After Christine had told him about Josephine, he'd thrown himself even more into repairs, hoping work would take away some of his grief, but it hadn't. The rest of the week had been a blur—Jo's memorial service, seeing Sandra and Christine crying by the grave, hugging each other. All of it reminded him of Dorothy's death.

He looked up through the glass dome, saw the circle of black sky and stars. He crossed the room to the beacon switch. He and Adam had installed it yesterday. They'd worked almost fourteen hours on the damned thing. Sandra and Christine had been helping for the past few days, too. Maybe, like him, they were using the lighthouse as a way to cope. They cleaned out rooms, swept, spackled walls—worked harder than he could because they were young.

Jake glanced around the room. It would take years to bring the lighthouse back to the way she'd been, but the electrical work was finished, the stairs safe, and the holes patched. As Sandra had pointed out, someone could even live here if they wanted to.

Jake looked at the new light switch. Like a kid, he held his breath and anticipated the flow of light. This is what Dorothy had wanted most of all. He clicked the switch.

The room remained dark.

Damn it.

The beacon had worked when Adam tried it. Frustrated, he snapped the switch twice.

His stomach twisted into a knot, and he stared at the beacon. Dorothy had talked about the beacon so many times. He shook his head, walked outside to the bench, closed his eyes, then opened them slowly, hoping she'd appear. He'd been waiting for days to see her, even if it was for just a split second. But tonight there was only the darkness he'd now become so used to, the shadowy trees, the ocean's rushing sound and the lighthouse looming overhead.

Angry and tired, he walked across the grass to the edge of the street, stopping at the sidewalk and turning around.

The lighthouse stood tall against the dark sky. How could he leave? This was Dorothy's favorite place and now it was his because here, at least, he felt alive. He walked back to the bench, sat and crossed his arms. Tonight he would work on the switch, maybe find out what was wrong. If not, tomorrow, early, he'd call Adam and get him to come down. The kid was a genius when it came to wiring, and he seemed to like working on the place.

Hey!

Jake startled at the sound, then smiled at hearing Dorothy's voice. "Thank God," he whispered, then looked all around.

Nothing.

His heart broke again and again. Deep down, he knew he wasn't going to see her.

"I'm proud of myself," I say, walking into Sandra's living room, actually feeling happy for the first time in weeks.

"That's good, I'm proud of you, too. Always have been." Sandra smiles. She is sitting on the couch next to Adam. They're holding hands, and the sight warms my heart. "What have you done? Brought world peace to San Pedro?"

"No. I finally made up my mind. I'm moving back here, and I found a real estate office that I can work out of."

"Great." Adam gets up and shakes my hand. "Congratulations. I know you'll be happy, and Sandra will really love it that you're here."

I sit down beside Sandra, smile.

"This is good news," she says. "I think you'll be happy here."

"I called my friend in Tucson, she's meeting the movers in a week, and they'll bring my car. They claim I'll have everything in fourteen days. I can put my stuff in storage when it gets here, if I don't have a place."

"What about your real estate job?"

"I'm giving Kathy a percentage of my listings. She'll handle everything. I'll still make money. And I've saved a few dollars."

"When do you start work?" Adam asks.

"After the boards next month. I'll do office hours, build my clientele. The owner says the market is great."

"You can live with me, if you want." Sandra gestures back to the bedrooms.

I look at Adam, who is now sitting in Josephine's chair. He is gazing at Sandra with a look of pure adoration.

"I think someone else will be living here soon."

Sandra winks at Adam. "Oh, you do, do you? You must know more than I do."

"Anyway, I'll stay with Dad till I find something."

"He seems better," Adam says. "I think the vibes from the lighthouse are helping him. And what he's accomplished, hell, that's got to make him feel better."

"*Vibes?*" I look at Adam to see if he's joking. He doesn't seem to be.

"Yeah. The lighthouse brought people home safely for years, took care of travelers, sailors. That was its job. We're all just sailing through this world.

The vibes are good at the lighthouse, maybe they healed your father's sorrow."

Sandra shakes her head. "Aren't you sorry you asked?"

Adam gets up, leans over Sandra and kisses her on the cheek. "I'm glad you put up with my weirdness. That's good." He touches her hair, just for a moment. "I'm going to go help Jake and absorb some good vibes, then get some work finished at my office. You need me to bring you anything? Good vibes, rocky-road ice cream, a diamond in the rough?"

Sandra shakes her head. "Not a thing."

Adam walks out the front door. Sandra and I move to the kitchen where the sun has warmed the room. We sit across from each other in the booth.

"So…" I say.

"So?"

"You know, how are you?"

"I'm okay." She spreads her fingers in front of her, studies her nails. "But I miss going up to the nursing home. I never thought I would. And I don't have to tell you how much I miss Mama."

"I know the feeling well."

She studies me, then clears her throat. "Tine, the other night, I had this dream about Mama. She was young and pretty, like when we were kids, standing in the backyard. Do you remember how she always did that, and your mother was out there, too? They had their arms around each other, like they were getting their picture taken. The dream woke me up, it was so real. I almost got up, went to the window and looked to see if they were actually out there."

I lean forward but don't say anything.

"I felt happy just seeing her, a happiness so deep that I can't describe it. She looked healthy, the light was back in her eyes, and I realized later I wouldn't want her to be the way she was, so sick."

I savor the idea that my mother might be with Josephine. "I wish I'd had a dream like that. You're lucky to have that to remember."

We sit for a moment, silent.

Sandra smiles at me. "Do you want to know about Adam?"

I smile.

"You're too nice to ask, right?" she says.

"Well yeah, I've been wondering what's going on, but I don't want to be nosy."

"We're spending a lot of time together, and I really like him."

"You more than like him, kiddo. I can see it when the two of you are together. The way you look at each other—"

"Even with his weirdness, being with him is so refreshing. Plus, he's romantic."

"Romance is good. I haven't had romance in so long I wouldn't know it if it hit me in the face. What does it feel like?"

"Well, I...what does it feel like?" She glances out the window, as if looking for the answer, then looks back, smiles. "It feels like I'm loved. You know? This is strange, but I think my mother was waiting for me to find Adam before she died. I had that feeling this morning. Being with him is like I have love again. When Mama was so sick, I didn't feel that way."

I know what she means—being loved is such a good thing to feel. "I'm happy for you."

"When Mama died, I felt so alone. At least you still have your father."

"I guess that should comfort me, but—"

"Tine, he loves you. He just has a funny way of showing it."

"Or not showing it." I laugh. "I've never thought my father even wanted me around."

"Out of all of us, I think gruff old Jake needs love the most."

My mom had said similar things. "Did you hear that from my mother?"

"Probably. She told me your father had a pretty rough childhood. Maybe that's why she never gave up on him."

I can almost hear my mother's soft voice, *He needs us, Chrissy.*

"It's weird the way everything is fitting together." Sandra breaks into my thoughts. "If you hadn't come back, I wouldn't have met Adam."

"I'm not sure I believe that. I think you two would have found each other somehow."

"But doesn't it seem like it's all meant to be?"

"I haven't had that epiphany yet. You need any help around here?" I gesture to the kitchen, but I mean the entire house, Josephine's things.

"I'm okay in that department. I cleaned out

more stuff, gave it to charity. Someone will get use out of it and that makes me happy." Sandra gets up and goes over to the sink, fills a glass with water, holds it against her chest.

When she turns around I see she's fighting tears.

"You're *not* okay."

"There are just these moments where I think my heart is going to break."

"My grief used to come in waves. I'd hear a song, or think of something Mom said, then I'd cry and feel better. Never knew when it would happen again."

"How did you do when you cleaned out her closet and dresser?" Sandra asks.

"I didn't get rid of everything. Most of her clothes I took to Goodwill, and I threw away her face creams, makeup. I didn't want anyone else touching those. It was cathartic, but it was difficult."

Sandra sits down at the table, sighs. "Funny thing. Life keeps going on. People still go to work, come home. I sit here sometimes and wonder who's living in Mama's room at the nursing home now. Death is like taking your hand out of water, there's a gap, but it fills up so quickly."

"Yeah, whether you want it to or not." And suddenly I realize the intense grief that has held me hostage for so long is gone.

I've come home from Sandra's. I stayed late and now it's dark. I swear there is still the faint scent of Obsession in this kitchen, but then again, maybe it's my imagination.

Dad walks in from the living room, stops at the table. "What are you doing?" he asks, not looking at me.

"I just got back from Sandra's."

"How is she?"

"She's crying a little."

He crosses his arms, nods, then looks out the kitchen window.

"What are you up to?" I ask.

"I'm not sure." He looks back, tired, distracted.

"Dad?"

"Yeah?"

"I've decided to stay."

He acknowledges my announcement with another nod.

"I want to live in San Pedro. Is it still all right if I stay at the house for a while?"

"Yeah, fine."

"I know you're sick of this question, but are you okay?"

"I'm going back to the lighthouse for a few hours. The beacon should turn on after all the work Adam and I did, but it doesn't. Something's wrong."

"It's so late, maybe you should rest. Isn't everything that needs to be up to code?"

He places his hands on the table, leans forward a little. "I just want the lighthouse to be finished, for it to be perfect. Your mother's dream was to have that light come on. It's the least I can do for her."

"But you're wearing yourself out."

"Christine, I feel better when I'm alone at the lighthouse. That's why I go there."

His words dance between us, skip against my heart and damage it a little more. As his expression grows more exhausted, I drop my gaze, stare at the table, because it's too painful to look at him.

"What else would make you happy, me not moving here?"

"One day you turn around and it's all over."

I look up. "What's all over?"

"Nothing." He shakes his head, presses his lips together.

Worry wells up inside me because I'm pretty sure I know what he means. "Are you talking about your life being over?"

"My grief isn't getting better, I'm worse."

For the first time, I realize just how depressed he is. "Mom would want us to go on, not feel sad, not stop our lives."

"That's not so easy." He straightens, his arms hanging at his sides, and I can feel his depression.

"Dad, how can I help you?"

"There are times…" He stops, takes a deep breath. I put my hand on his shoulder. He's trembling and this scares me.

"There are times *what?*"

"I don't think I can go on."

His words plunge me into a deep fog. It takes me a few moments to understand what he's said.

"Can't go on? What do you mean?" But before I can say another word, he walks out the back door.

Jake looked down at the cliffs. Without moonlight or his flashlight, he couldn't see the waves crashing against the rocks, but he could hear them. He'd come to the park an hour ago, told himself he was going to do more work on the beacon, but he knew he wasn't.

He sucked in a breath, leaned over the railing and felt the wind rushing against his face. He didn't know what to do or where his life was going. And more confusion and grief attacked his mind and body.

Why couldn't he just go on? Trust that his life would be okay someday. But trusting in something he couldn't see or touch was the hardest for him. It was the same when he was flying on instruments—he had to force himself to believe. He was never good at doing that. Since he was a kid, he liked everything straightforward and mapped out. Yet, night after night for years, he flew successful flights, landed between the lights of the runway. Why couldn't he do that now? Why couldn't he go along and live what was left of his life?

The wind whipped around him and pushed him back a little, but he held on to the cold railing.

He turned and glanced back, beyond the park. The bleached streetlights gave the area a foggy appearance. He brought his attention around to the cliffs. He'd never really thought about how far down it was. From the lookout point to the rocky point below it had to be at least a hundred and twenty feet—all jagged edges, no sand.

Jake looked up, studied the dark sky with all its stars.

God, the world was beautiful.

Dorothy had loved the night air and evenings when they used to walk. She'd take his hand, hold it as they strolled along, and he'd listen to their breathing, the only sound that mattered.

"Where are you?" he yelled. The wind lifted his words and broke them apart. He wanted to fill up with faith. He needed to believe in life, in the way Dorothy had wanted him to, but he couldn't.

He had never had much faith. At eight, he'd tried to believe that his mother hadn't meant to bash a teakettle against his cheekbone, but when she'd gone and gotten the broomstick and brought it down on his back, he knew she hated him. And when it took his mother two weeks to walk him to the doctor—his cheek black and blue, his eye swollen shut—the rest of his faith disappeared.

So why did he think he could wish Dorothy back? The few nights he'd seen her were only his imagination and grief, like the invisible undertow, pulling him back.

"No!" he whispered.

Seeing her was real and no one could take that away from him. No one.

He looked at the sky again and wished he were flying far above the earth, detached from the constant ache he felt.

Flying?

He was a grieving fool with too many regrets, getting older and more foolish with each moment. He looked over the railing.

It would be so easy....

The wind gusted more, curled under him and blew him back a little. He pushed forward, climbed over the metal bars and stood on the edge of the rocky cliff.

He wanted to feel like he used to, free, without pain, in control, loved. He slung his arms out like wings. The wind ruffled his shirt. Below blackness lined with white licked the earth.

So easy....

Adrenaline seeped into his muscles, making him feel like he was on fire. A thick swell of anguish gushed through him as he thought about Dorothy, alone in her car. Why hadn't he gone with her?

Too many memories to hold back.

He turned slightly and caught sight of the lighthouse. It stood quietly against the dark sky. Dorothy had once said she loved the way it never gave up on anyone. He took a step, wished the wind would lift him up, pull him into the air.

"Hey."

Jake turned, stumbled forward a little, away from the cliff.

Christine was standing at the railing, holding her mother's flashlight. The look on her face cut him to the bone.

"Dad, please come home. Mom's real dream was for us to get along."

"Dad, what are you doing?"

My heart beats hard into my throat. I watch as he walks to the railing and climbs over it. When he's on my side I throw my arms around his neck, begin crying.

"What were you doing out there?" I pull back, look at him, then wipe my eyes. I remember what he said in the kitchen, how his life is over, and worry and anger swirl in my chest like the ocean far below. I shine Mom's light in his face. He squints, looks so sad and lost some of my anger breaks off, drifts away.

"Don't you understand you're *all* I have?" I grab his arm and shake it. "I've tried to be a good daughter so you'll like me, so you'll be my father, but nothing seems to work."

He stares at me as if he's trying to understand what I've just said, then his expression crumbles and he begins to cry, too.

"Dad?"

"It's not you…your mother knew. It's me. That's why I stayed back, let her do everything."

I understand what he is saying, but it doesn't make it easier to hear. "But why were you out there?"

He rubs his face, looks toward the cliff. "I thought I saw your mother."

"What?" Then I play back what he just said. "You thought you *saw* Mom?" I take a deep breath.

"Yeah."

"You saw someone who looks like her?"

"No, I saw her."

"For how long?" I stare at him.

"A second."

"Just tonight?"

He looks at the lighthouse, then me. "Yeah."

My whole body tightens with worry, then I remember the dream Sandra had, how it made her feel okay about her mother's death. I take his hand—his fingers are so cold.

"Maybe what you saw was like a dream. Sandra had a dream about Josephine that felt real. Josephine and Mom were together. That's when Sandra knew her mother was okay. Maybe it was like that."

The wind whips around us.

"Yeah, that was probably it," he finally says.

"Mom would want us to know she's okay. She wouldn't want us to go on worrying or grieving forever."

He nods.

"We have to believe that."

"Yeah."

The wind pushes us toward each other.

He sits on the bench, his hands on his thighs, and he stares at the ground.

"Dad…." I stop, don't know what else to say.

The night is so quiet. I sit next to him, hear the ocean rushing and the leaves rustling in the trees.

He looks at me. Even in the dim light I can see that tears have streaked his face.

"Dad, you need to go see someone, maybe your doctor, or someone. You can't handle this depression alone. And I can't handle it for you."

He nods, presses his lips together. "Maybe I should."

"You need to go." I think about him on the cliff and my heart beats harder.

He takes a deep breath. "A daughter shouldn't have to worry about her father," he says.

"But that's a part of life. You'd worry about me."

He shakes his head. "I haven't treated you like I've always wanted to. I was afraid I wouldn't be a good father, so I stayed back. That wasn't right." He crosses his arms. "But I'll try to do better."

He stands and looks at me. And with his words I feel a warmth inside my chest—a feeling that we have connected a little.

"I'll go see someone so you won't worry." Dad rubs his eyes, sighs. "I guess I need some help to get through this." He walks a few feet toward the lighthouse then stops and looks back to me.

"We'd better go home now. You're probably tired," he says, waits for me.

I stand, go over to my father, and we begin our quiet walk home.

EPILOGUE

I'm sitting on the couch, looking at the eight-foot Christmas tree I just decorated and I'm thinking about how life is so unpredictable.

It's only December 7, but I've just finished putting all of Mom's red-and-white Santas on the real Scotch pine. Three days ago, I told Dad I was excited about the holidays and I wanted a real tree this year. Yesterday he surprised me with this one. Maybe it's too early to decorate, but I don't care. The living room smells like a pine forest. A little while ago, I put on a Bing Crosby Christmas album, and I'm having hot chocolate.

We both agreed we don't know where the time has gone. Almost two years have passed since my mother's accident. I'm living in our house and Dad is settled in the lighthouse. Last summer, he cleaned up the living area, then added a small kitchen and moved in August 23, my mother's birthday. I begged him not to move, but he insisted, saying we both needed space.

Some things never change.

For a long time after he moved, I worried about him down at the lighthouse all alone. I'd walk to the park every morning to make sure he was okay, and he always was. By September, when people started coming to look at the lighthouse, I noticed he was smiling a little. And then, in October, he seemed happy sometimes, so I quit fretting so much. Over the past year, I've learned when my father has made up his mind, well, that's it.

But we do try to help each other, like him bringing the tree over, and me cooking for the holidays. At Thanksgiving, after Chet, Sandra and Adam left, I asked Dad if he'd seen Mom anymore. He shook his head. I guess we've both moved on in our own ways. Then Dad said talking to someone, and me being here, have helped.

I'm not doing too badly myself. The real estate office I work at is downtown on Pacific Avenue in a building that used to be Lorine's Dress Shop. My mother bought her clothes there. Every morning, when I walk through the door, I think of her, the way she dressed, but this doesn't make me sad.

San Pedro real estate is still booming. I'm always trying to find the right houses for my clients. At times, it doesn't seem like the perfect place will ever surface, and clients lose hope, but I tell them, hold on, things will change. Then all of a sudden, when we least expect it, a great house comes on the market and they're happy.

Life is like that, too. One day it feels like things can't get any worse and then, a moment later, problems begin to disappear and life is better.

I'm dating, so I guess anything can change. I met Steven through the Real Estate Association. He looks like a middle-aged Kirk Douglas. He's a top-performing Realtor—a nice guy. Steven and I have been out five times, and maybe it will turn into something. He's not perfect, but who is?

Adam and Sandra are living together. They make great neighbors. I go over for dinner a lot, and Dad has joined us twice. I've taken Steven over once. Sandra and I still share memories about our mothers, but my hurt has lessened, and I think hers has, too. One day this summer, I cut across our backyards barefoot to join Sandra for a margarita, and I thought about Mom traveling the same path. When I went into the kitchen, I felt like her for just a moment, so hopeful.

About six months ago the *L.A. Times* did a story on the lighthouse and my father, Pilot Navigates Lighthouse Restoration. The Associated Press picked it up and people from all over sent him money. Of course this pissed Dad off, and he announced he was "no damned charity." But Sandra talked him into forming the Lighthouse Society. She's spearheading it and doing one hell of a job.

Dad talks about how the lighthouse will never be finished. He complains about the constant repairs, but he hasn't been working as hard as he did when he began. I think the work has helped him come to terms with Mom's death. And when he shows people the beacon, he smiles, then leads them to my mother's plaque. The plaque is in the front, by the gate. It's small, a replica of the lighthouse with just three words printed on it:

Believe
For Dorothy

Dad, after he had it made, asked me to come to the lighthouse one afternoon. It was one of those days my mother would have loved—clear blue sky, a slight breeze, and I felt the world's perfection. He showed me the plaque and I hugged him, then we put it up, no fanfare, just he and I, not talking, but honoring someone we both loved. Every time I look at it, I imagine how happy my mother would be that my father and I are trying to be friends.

This summer, a few locals came to the park right before sunset for a picnic. They waited for the lighthouse beacon to come on. When it did, I heard a sigh, a couple of *heys* and someone said, *Can you believe that?* And I whispered to myself, *Yes, I can.*

REQUEST YOUR FREE BOOKS!

2 FREE NOVELS TO INTRODUCE YOU TO OUR BRAND-NEW LINE!

There's the life you planned. And there's what comes next.

NEXT05